THE SPIRIT OF St. ANDREW

ROBERT.J. DONALD

Copyright © 2024 ROBERT.J. DONALD

All rights reserved.

DEDICATION

I think it only right that I dedicate my work to the two most

important women throughout my life as well as my three children and grandchildren.

Firstly, to my loving and long-suffering wife of 52 years Helen. Long suffering in the fact that, once I get my head down and start to write I am oblivious of everyone around me including my wife, yet she never complains.

Secondly, my mother who always said I should be a writer and many of the stories she disclosed, from my family's past, I went on to make use of.

Finally, my children (it seems strange referring to them as children as they are all well into their forties and early fifties)

who all do nothing but encourage me and believe in my work.

Thank you to all of you.

Table of Contents

- **CHAPTER 1.** 10
  - REMEMBERING. 10
- **CHAPTER 2.** 31
  - BACK FROM THE DEAD. 31
- **CHAPTER 3.** 38
  - A CALL TO BARRACKS. 38
- **CHAPTER 4.** 52
  - FRANCE. 52
- **CHAPTER 5.** 63
  - OVER THE TOP. 63
- **CHAPTER 6.** 84
  - BAD NEWS. 84
- **CHAPTER 7.** 92
  - GOING HOME. 92
- **CHAPTER 8.** 99
  - THE WEDDING. 99
- **CHAPTER 9.** 113
  - SHORE LEAVE. 113
- **CHAPTER 10.** 125
  - MURDER. 125
- **CHAPTER 11.** 135
  - TRIAL. 135
- **CHAPTER 12.** 142
  - THE HELLHOLE. 142
- **CHAPTER 13.** 160
  - EXECUTION. 160
- **CHAPTER 14.** 168
  - CAPTIVES. 168

CHAPTER 15.	181
VISITING.	181
CHAPTER 16.	185
LIFE WITH THE YANOMAMI.	185
CHAPTER 17.	214
GOODBYE TO THE YANOMAMI.	214
CHAPTER 18.	222
LIFE ON THE RIVER.	222
CHAPTER 19.	242
INTO THE OCEAN.	242
CHAPTER 20.	248
OUT OF THE FRYING PAN.	248
CHAPTER 21.	255
A HELPING HAND.	255
CHAPTER 22.	257
BOSTON.	257
CHAPTER 23.	267
HOME AT LAST.	267
Chapter 24.	271
RUNNING FOR YOUR LIFE.	271
CHAPTER 25.	282
FLYING HIGH.	282
CHAPTER 26.	304
A FLIGHT TO FREEDOM.	304

CHAPTER 1.
REMEMBERING.

David Harley was trying hard to open his eyes. This six-foot blonde-haired Scotsman, known as Davie to all who knew him, was aware he was on his back as his eyes eventually flickered open. Next thing was focus, as he blinked several times before realizing, he was in a bed, with other beds at either side of him. Jesus, he thought, I'm in a bloody hospital. Before Davie knew it, he was wiggling his fingers, then his toes, to make sure everything was there and was working. He was relieved to find out they were, but he soon became aware of a pounding headache which also made him realize that his head was indeed bandaged.

"Ah, you are awake soldier, and what prey is your name?" Said a young nurse in a French accent as she felt to check his pulse.

"My name......?" Quizzed Davie, in a way that was saying, why, don't you have my name.

Oie soldier......your name?"

"It's David Harley." Replied Davie.

"Good David, I'll pass that on."

"So, nurse, how the hell did I get here?"

"You don't remember?" Asked the nurse, to which Davie just slowly shook his head.

"You, Mister Harley, are a casualty of the battle at the Somme district and to all intent and purposes you are one of the lucky ones, many soldiers perished."

Davies face twisted, "My head..." He said, "... it's throbbing."

"I'm not surprised you were hit by shrapnel just behind your ear, I'll get you two aspirin, that will help relieve the pain."

The nurse left leaving Davie to try and gather his thoughts as he closed his eyes once more. As he wondered what the hell he was doing in this place as he suddenly remembered the day in his life that started his journey into the great war.

The Spirit of St. Andrew

It was the day his beloved wife Jean passed away. She had died in childbirth delivering them of a healthy baby boy, sister to his three-year-old daughter Helen. Jean had bled internally, and they had no way of stopping it.

Davie remembered sitting in a chair at Jeans bedside staring at her lifeless body, his newborn son sleeping in the family cot beside him. Davie was inconsolable as he then stared at the tin bath beside him which was near to full of blood-soaked sheets and towels. Jean was a beautiful woman in her mid-twenties, with long flowing red hair which for now was flat to her head, wet from the sweat she had perspired while undergoing her ordeal.

Davies constant gaze was suddenly disturbed when his mother Susan entered the bedroom with a cup of tea in hand. She was a slim, attractive woman, in her late fifties, with greying short-cut hair, which still had streaks of her original blonde running through it.

"Davie son, I've brought you a cuppy, you've been sat there for hours. Why don't you come through and have some breakfast." She pleaded softly.

Davies tears ran down his face, "Look at her Mum, you would think I could give her a wee shake and she'd wake up."

Susan put her hand on his shoulder, "She's at peace Davie. You must take Solace from that."

Susan then went over to the bed Jean lay in and pulled the sheet up over her head to try and help her son draw closure on the tragic episode, before she turned once more to her son.

"Come on Davie, Cathy will be up shortly to feed the wee one. Come on, get some breakfast."

Cathy was Davies older sister by two years and had just three weeks previous, given birth to her second child a daughter named Susan after Davies mother. This would work out well as Cathy could wet nurse the new-born.

Davie staggered through to the kitchen where his father Jim was sitting by the fireside along with Davie's younger brother William or Wull, as they all referred to him. Jim had worked his days on Dryestanes, the family farm, and it had taken its toll. He suffered from TB and the fact he still puffed at his pipe didn't help matters as Susan constantly reminded him.

No words were spoken as Davie slumped into a kitchen chair. His pretty little three-year-old daughter Helen came and sat on his knee as he embraced her warmly.

"Where's mummy?" She enquired softly.

Davie tried to hold back the tears, "...She's just having a nice long sleep ma wee lamb."

His words seemed to appease the wee one as she cuddled into her father.

The kitchen was a good-sized area containing a large open fire which had an oven at either side and a kettle hung from a hook which could swivel back and forth from the fire. There was a fair-sized table which had half a dozen chairs around it. Davie was sat in one of these.

As Susan went to fetch Davie some porridge, Jim happened to glance out of the window which looked down the farm road that stretched a good hundred yards to two cottages at the end of the drive. One of these housed Cathy and her man Jack with their two children. The other cottage lay empty till such times as the farm need extra help, then, what was known as an extra man would fill it. Drystanes Farm had been in the family for over one hundred years and would be passed on to Davie in due time.

"Jesus......." Said Jim, ".......here comes the school missy (teacher), Jeans wee sister Fiona".

When the doctor left the house after Jean died, he had told them he would inform Jean's sister of her passing, as well as the local undertaker.

Fiona bore a very strong resemblance to her older sister. She was a year younger that Jean with the same flowing red hair and beautiful features. She had travelled by bicycled from the village of Dyce just two miles from Drystanes on what was a beautiful sunny April morning.

Susan met her at the door as she entered wearing a deep green two-piece suit consisting of a calf length skirt and waist length jacket. The others greeted her before she made her way over to Davie who stood to greet her.

"Oh, David I am so sorry, you must be heartbroken." She said as she embraced her brother-in-law. She then, to Davies consternation whispered in his ear, "I am here for you any time you want to take me."

Everyone was fighting back tears as Fiona then embraced them one by one. Last being young Wull, who himself had always had a huge crush for Fiona. Fiona then held Wull at arm's length as she stared into his face.

"My God......" She said slightly aghast, causing Wull to blush somewhat, "......surly this isn't young William. What a handsome young man you have developed into. My God David you will have competition here when you go looking for a new woman."

The others were slightly bemused by Fiona's words.

"Jesus Christ lassie, I hardly think Davie's on the hunt for a woman yet for God's sake, and ah think you better release Wull before he explodes." Snapped Jim.

Fiona released the red faced Wull, "You are right Mr Harley, how insensitive of me, I do apologise."

"Fiona....." said Susan, ".... would you like to see your sister?"

"Of course, Mrs. Harley." She replied, as Susan escorted Fiona to the bedroom where Jean lay.

As they left Davie rose from his chair, ignoring the bowl of porridge set down by his mother, laid wee Helen down beside her toys, and went over to the cupboard beside the window where he removed a bottle of whisky, lifted a class, and went to his bedroom.

It was around noon the next day that he emerged from his bedroom looking slightly the worse for wear having devoured most of the contents of the whisky bottles which he laid down on the kitchen table.

"Davie......" Said Susan softly, "..... I tried to wake you this morning. The thing is the undertaker came and took Jean to their rooms. You need to go there and find out about the arrangements."

Davie just nodded before slumping into a chair.

Back in France Davie's thoughts were disturbed by the same young nurse who asked him how his headache was, too which he replied, "a wee bit easier".

He then took hold of the nurse's arm, "Tell me...." he asked, "......are there any of my comrades left?"

The nurse looked at him solemnly, "There are a few, but I have to say many perished Mr Harley."

"I had a friend nurse......a Mr Goodison?" Davie asked.

The nurse sensing his pleading look said, "I'll try to find out.... now, please, you must rest."

Davie then lay back in his bed and once more retraced his journey to where he was.

Davie recalled going off the rails in a big way soon after Jean died. Come the day of her funeral he was, once more, the worse for whisky. The three days up to the funeral was a haze as far as Davie was concerned. He recalled his father losing his temper with him when, while at work in the fields and in a drunken state, he had left a gate open whereby several cows got out. One of the beasts run amok in Dyce village before being drought back to the farm. Fortunately, no one was harmed.

After Jeans commitment several friends and family gathered back at Drystanes for the wake. Davie just sat in a corner of the living room nursing another dram. The intensity of the people around him got to be to much as he got up and headed for the barn, whisky bottle in hand, just to be alone. The rain was pouring down as he made a dart for the cover of the barn. He parked himself on a bundle of straw and stared up at the roof, sipping from the bottle as he did. Considering the rain outside, he was surprised to hear someone approach.

"Who's there?" He called out.

"It's me......Fiona." She said, as she folded the umbrella, she had to shelter herself."

"Jesus Fiona....what the hell do you want." Snapped Davie.

"Charming." She responded.

Davie took a shake to himself, "I'm sorry Fiona......I'm just not good company at the moment."

"Apparently not......." She said as she closed in on him as he lay on the straw, "......you know you will get over this David, time is a great healer."

"Jesus......" said Davie, looking skyward, ".... if I hear someone tell me that one more time, I thing I'll bloody well shoot myself....and them!"

Fiona's response surprised Davie as she said, "Well then, why the hell don't you......"

Davie looked up towards Fiona, "Why the hell don't I what?"

"Shoot yourself......I mean I don't think I've ever seen anyone so pitiful, you're pathetic." She snapped.

Davie then sprang to his feet, "Now just you listen here Fiona I have just lost the one thing in my life I lived for. Maybe I have a right to be......what was it you said.... pitiful."

"Actually...." She responded coldly, ".......I said pathetic."

Davies anger rose as he found himself eye to eye with Fiona. As he stared at her, he suddenly felt he was staring into his Jeans eyes, such was the resemblance.

Fiona held her ground and stared back into Davies red rimmed eyes. As resourceful as Fiona was, she felt empathy towards Davie, a man she always had strong feelings for, despite him being her sister's man.

Before she realised, she found herself putting her arms around him, "You know David I meant what I said the day Jean died. I'm here for you whenever you want me."

That was all the invitation Davie needed as he kissed her full on the lips. It was a passionate lingering kiss which saw the pair sliding down on to the inviting bed of straw.

The Spirit of St. Andrew

Within seconds they were pulling at each other's clothing as the passionate kiss lingered. Before they knew it, they had seized the moment. Neither of them realizing what they were doing, nor caring it would seem, confident the rainstorm was keeping everyone at bay.

As soon as they had rolled apart and started to fix their clothing, Davie was the first to speak.

"Jesus Fiona, what the hell did we just do?"

"Well...." Replied Fiona sarcastically, ".......at least that's better than, how was it for you?"

Davie then dug a deeper hole for himself as he said, "Jesus Fiona we should never have done what we just did."

"My God David Harley you certainly know how to flatter a girl......" Snapped Fiona, ".... but don't you worry, no one will know of this but us two."

Davie struggled for words which always seemed to be the wrong ones.

"Look Fiona I just saw Jean in your eyes, I made a mistake......I mean, you and me......it just can't happen......I'm sorry."

"Jesus, you men are a pathetic lot. I could have helped you get over this David Harley.......still, that's a fine-looking young brother you've got there, maybe I could have better luck with him." Said Fiona provocatively.

Anger grew in Davie as he closed in on Fiona once more, "For God's sake Fiona, Wull is only eighteen, your eight years older than him......"

Fiona cut him off, "........He's all the man he'll ever be David....anyway, it could be fun seeing you squirm over your young brother."

Fiona then stormed away with Davie trying to stop her, but to no avail.

Davie jolted slightly when the nurse softly shook his arm to wake him from his sleep.

"I've brought someone to see you Mr Harley."

A tall dark-haired good-looking man stood over Davies bed; all be it supported by two crutches. It was Tam Goodison a man he befriended when he joined up.

"So, yer alive then." Tam said casually.

"Jesus Tam, it seems your alive as well." Replied Davie stating the obvious as he pushed himself up in his bed.

"You're wounded, Tam. They didnae shoot your balls off, did they?" Joked Davie.

"Cheeky bugger......." retorted Tam, ".......no, I was hit in the hip.... it'll mend."

Davie called the nurse as she made to leave, "Can I get up out o' here?"

"Perhaps tomorrow, if your well enough." She relied as she left.

"That's good news Davie. Probably get home the day after".

That night Davies thoughts returned to home once more. He recalled how badly he behaved after Jeans death. He remembered the following Sunday when he arrived late for Kirk. He sculked in at the back of the Kirk and remembered being annoyed when he saw Fiona sat beside Wull arm in arm. After the Kirk service the congregation all gathered outside where Wull was announcing to everyone that Fiona had promised him the first dance in the village hall due the following Saturday.

This caused Davie to confront Fiona as she prepared to head home. Davie caught up with her and pulled at her arm, causing her to turn.

"What the hell are you playing at Fiona?" He asked briskly.

Fiona pulled her arm away, "What the hell are you talking about David?" She demanded.

"Young Wull, that's what I'm talking about......Jesus' woman he's only eighteen and he's daft on you......and you know it."

Fiona smiled at Davie, "Do I detect a hint of jealousy Mr Harley?"

"Don't play games Fiona......just.... just, leave him alone."

"You know David, I gave myself to you that day in the barn and you snubbed me. That, after I told you I was there for you if you wanted me. The thing is that's twice you rejected me......nobody, gets a third chance with me......so......as you now know, I have moved on to your handsome young brother......" Fiona then went in close to Davie's face, "........so learn to live with it!"

That night, once again Davie hit the whisky bottle and spoke to no one. Next morning, being the Monday, he rose early and to his mother's surprise was all dressed up in his good suit.

"My......" Said his mother, "......where the devil are you off to all dressed up?"

"Aberdeen......" Said Davie before adding, "......and I may be a couple of days."

Susan's mind went to the war raging in Europe, "Jesus Davie, don't be going and doing anything stupid."

Davie then looked into his mother's eyes and almost became tearful, "the thing is mum since Jean died, I can't get myself together. Everywhere I go on the farm I see her running across the fields to me, her hair blowing in the wind. In bed at night, I stare at the empty pillow beside me and I see her face. Then I put my hand out and she's gone. It's driving me mad mum and I need a bit of time to myself to see if I can get my head around it."

"I understand son......just don't do anything hasty, is all I'm saying."

The nurse approached Davie as he sat on the edge of his bed. He was surprised to see an officer with her, a captain he recognised but did not know his name. The nurse told him that this was Private Harley and left.

"At last," said the captain, " we can put a name to the face."

"I don't understand Sir." Said a bemused Davie.

"The thing is Harley when you were found in no man's land after the assault, the stretcher bearers thought that you were dead and laid you in the line of bodies, removing your papers as they did so....." The captain drew a breath, "......the thing is Harley they then sent word back to your family that you were KIA. It wasn't until they went to bury you one of the men saw you move and, well, here you are......"

"What......" Snapped Davie, "......you mean my family think I'm dead."

"Afraid so old boy. But don't worry, we'll soon rectify that now that we know who you are."

Davie slumped back on to his bed and gave thought to the fact that this would be even worse news for his mother than the day he returned from Aberdeen to tell her he had joined up.

It was early evening, two days since Davie set of for Aberdeen. Jim and Susan were sitting by the kitchen fire when the front door burst open. It was Davie and he was definitely the worse for drink. He suddenly jumped to attention and clicked his heels as all eyes focused on him. He then gave a salute with his right hand and said, "Private David Harley at his majesties service!"

"What!" shouted Susan as her jaw hit the floor.

"That's right mother, I have taken the Kings shilling." explained a now grinning Davie.

The Spirit of St. Andrew

"Davie are you mad......Jesus you're exempt from all that madness over there, you're a land worker....... oh God, please tell me you're joking?" Pleaded Susan.

"Never been more serious in all my life mother......and now, this soldier needs some sleep." Was all he said as he made for his bedroom.

It was the weekend of the village dance. As usual there was a very good turnout. All the Harleys were there except for Davie and Cathy's man, Jack. Jack had got himself a bit of a reputation some years ago as a bit of a ladies' man. Not trusting himself fully he had told Cathy he would stay home and watch the bairns.

The band was a gathering of musicians from the village, consisting of two accordions, two fiddles a double base and a drummer. Scottish country music and dance was the order of the day as everyone started to settle in.

All that was except young Wull who was looking around frantically for Fiona who had yet to arrive.

As Fiona approached the hall, she was taken by a very dark looking character standing back by a lamp post just outside the hall. Although dark in feature he was a very good-looking man of around Fiona's own age, wearing a black suit to match his image. She was sure she had seen him around the village of late but never found out just who he was. As he smiled in her direction, Fiona turned away and entered the hall her mind still wondering as to who this man was.

As she entered the hall all eyes seemed to divert towards her as she looked quite ravishing in a low cut dark blue calf length dress. Her red hair was tied up showing of her swan-like neck adorned with a black choker which had a single pearl dangling in the centre. Wives were digging their men with their elbows to get them to avert their stare somewhere else.

As soon as Wull set his eyes on her he was off across the hall like a little puppy that had just caught site of its mother.

Arriving at Fiona she had to raise a hand to stop him in his tracks.

"William, how wonderful to see you." She said with a smile.

"Thankyou......" he said gleefully, "......you look beautiful Fiona."

"Why thankyou William you look quite dashing yourself. I hope you are over to ask me for that dance I promised you?"

"Off course." He replied as they walked out on to the middle of the hall for the opening waltz."

The Spirit of St. Andrew

As the evening progressed Fiona was becoming somewhat weary of Wulls constant attention. She was close to telling him where to go when something happened at the other side of the hall. A group had gathered round someone lying on the floor, it was Jim, Wulls father, who had taken one of his turns.

Susan was calling out for people to stand back and give him room to breathe.

As Wull approached, Cathy instructed him to get the horse and cart and bring it to the door. As Wull went he was full of apologies to Fiona for having to leave her for the night. She for her part was relieved as he was becoming just to overbearing with his constant fawning over her with praise and apologies every time he moved or turned the wrong way.

Before the Harleys left, everyone was pleased to see Jim was on his feet and making the usual protestations that he was alright with Susan demanding that he goes home right away.

After they left, the band played the last waltz to a rather depleted audience, Fiona being amongst the last to leave.

It was a fairly warm late April night as Fiona strolled alone through the dark streets, lit only by a few rather dull gas lamps. She felt a slight unease as she went, feeling sure someone was behind her. She stopped and turned quickly and was given a start when she came face to face with the dark stranger she saw earlier.

"Jesus......" she called out, "......are you following me?"

The man held up two stopping hands, "Sorry......" he said apologetically, ".......I was just making sure you got home safely."

Fiona relaxed slightly, "Well Sir, the only thing making me feel unsafe is your presence......who the hell are you anyway?"

"Alex Findley, at your service." He said with a slight bow of his head.

Fiona squinted her face, "I've seen you around I'm sure, but I know you're not local......"

Alex interrupted, "No, I live with my aunt in a farm cottage just to the north of the village."

"So why didn't you come into the dance Mr Findley?"

Alex shrugged his shoulders, "Oh, I'm just not to fond of crowds I guess, but I could see from outside that you were being hit on by some young upstart."

"...and a fine handsome young man he is too." Fiona teased.

"Perhaps......" said Alex before continuing, ".... but I don't see him being enough man, for you."

Fiona smiled at the thought of her new associate sounding a little jealous of young William.

Fiona smiled, "....and you would be enough man, would you Mr Findlay?"

"I've had my moments." replied Alex, boasting a little.

Fiona leered slightly, "I'm afraid this lady would need a little more than a moment."

Alex didn't answer, rather he changed tack, "Look, it's getting late. Can I walk you to your house......to see you home safely is all I mean."

Fiona looked into his dark eyes for a second, then smiled, "I suppose an escort on a dark night wouldn't go amiss."

The two walked on together.

CHAPTER 2.
BACK FROM THE DEAD.

Tam Goodison was sitting on Davies bed beside him.

"Jesus Tam......." said Dave dolefully, ".......my poor mother is in for a shock when she hears I've been killed."

"Aye Davie and an even bigger one when she finds out your still alive." Replied Tam.

Davie nodded then twisted his face, "Wait a minute Tam, they've only just found out who I am here. That telegram saying I'm alive won't be away to my mother yet......."

"....and?" Quizzed Tam.

"And........" came back Davie, "......if, as that captain said I am off home as soon as possible, I could get home just as quick as the telegram......now that, would fairly surprise the hell out o' everybody!"

The Spirit of St. Andrew

Tam went back to his ward as Davie returned to laying on his bed and reminiscing about home.

The Sunday morning after the village dance found Fiona lying on her bed gazing at the man sleeping beside her. She had allowed the dark stranger Alex Findley into her bed. She thought him a little on the rough side, but in her mind gave him a pass mark, just like the teacher she was. It also crossed her mind what the Ladies of the village would think if they found out their school Missy was fornicating with a dark stranger.

Later that morning she found herself at the Kirk where Wull, to her slight annoyance, was still apologising for leaving her the night before.

She had to confess to herself that she was glad to hear that his father was a little better after his turn, the previous night.

Davie had also gone along to the Kirk and was soon confronted by Fiona after the service.

"You didn't go to the dance last night David. I would have given you a dance." She said, probingly.

"I don't think I'm much company these days Fiona." He replied dolefully.

"Well, I certainly got plenty dances from your handsome young brother." She teased.

Davies mood changed, "Fiona, I've asked you to leave Wull alone."

"I would David, if you'd only let me in, I could sooth all your aches and pains your heart is going through." Said Fiona, surprising Davie with her compassionate plea.

Davie then grinned, which annoyed Fiona slightly.

"I'm afraid you're too late for all that Fiona..." said Davie, as Fiona then interrupted.

".... but why David, why?"

Davie then looked Fiona square in the eye, "......because I've enlisted!"

Fiona took a shocked step back, "Enlisted!......are you mad? Have you any idea the rate men are being killed at out there."

Davie then stared skyward, "Why the hell is everyone so sure I'll be killed out there......Jesus!"

Fiona then shook her head, still trying to come to terms with what Davie had just told her.

"You know David, perhaps it's not a bad thing you going over there and getting your head blown off......" She said, pausing for him to query, which he did.

"....and why would that be Fiona?"

"Because I'll be able to pursue your young brother and have him all to myself, along with your precious farm." She said teasing at Davie.

His face twisted, as all sorts entered his mind, causing him to ask quizzically, ".... the farm?"

Fiona then closed in on Davie and stared into his eyes, ".... Yes David, the farm.......I mean I saw your father last night, lovely man though he is, but he hasn't long for this world, and with you getting yourself killed out in France......well, that leaves the farm to my darling William......and I'll soon persuade him to sell up.......should fetch a pretty penny I wouldn't wonder."

Davie's chin had dropped, before he came to, "Why you are a conniving little bitch, my family would never allow that to happen."

A group of Kirk attendee's including Davie's family were starting to break up and head home. As they did young Wull started to make his way over to Davie and Fiona.

"Ah......" said Fiona, "...I see your young brother approaching, he's invited me to go walking up by the standing stones. I'm afraid we can't have you coming along and playing gooseberry now, can we David."

Davie just growled to himself and walked away.

Later that day Fiona returned to her home or rather her two rooms which was within the domain of the good doctor Munro, who allowed the rooms to be let out free of charge to whoever was the school mistress at the time.

Fiona was slightly surprised to find that Alex Findley was still there.

"Goodness, I'd have thought you'd have left by now?" She quizzed.

Alex was stood against the small kitchen sink as he replied, "Actually I did go out, I saw you and that young upstart head for the standing stones......very cozy."

"My my......" said Fiona with a slight smirk, "......do I detect a hint of jealousy?"

"Not jealousy......more curiosity, I mean what the hell can you see in him?" Asked Alex as he closed in on Fiona.

"Oh, I have my reasons, which I may or may not let you into some day." Teased Fiona.

The Spirit of St. Andrew

That same day Jim was sitting on the bench at the back of the Dryestanes farmhouse throwing breadcrumbs to the ducks in the pond when Davie sat down beside him.

"How are you, Dad?" Asked Davie a slight concern to his voice.

"Och, no lang for this world now son." Replied Jim dolefully.

"Here....." snapped Davie, "....we'll hae less oh that kind o' talk......you've years in you yet."

Jim glanced round at his son, ".... if you're goin' tae sit there and haver shite tae me ye may as well away back inside."

Davie didn't respond other than to grip his hand on his father's shoulder and smile into his face.

"Actually, Davie I'm glad we've got a minute together, there's something I need to tell you...."

"What's that dad?"

"This'll make it just you and your mother who know what I'm about to say. The thing is Davie earlier this week I changed my will......" said Jim, causing Davie to interrupt.

"Jesus dad, what for, I mea......."

Davie was stopped by his fathers raised hand.

"Just listen......" snapped Jim, causing Davie to relent. "......I know your being kind saying I've got a lot o' time yet, but I know my own body.... and..... well......it's fucked, plain and simple."

Davie bowed his head and gave way with a slight smile at his father's honesty.

"Thing is Davie we you going' off tae war........" Jim realising Davie was about to object held up a stopping hand. "......I know what yer goin' tae say son about no getting' yersel' killed out there and I prey to the almighty that you don't. Yet, in the event that you do, and that I pass as well, that would leave the farm to young Wull. The thing is Davie I think he'll just be too young to handle all that responsibility......"

"So....?" Went Davie.

"So... I've put a clause into my will that Wull won't get the farm until he's twenty-one and that your mother along with Cathy's man Jack will run things till then."

Davie could see the sense in his father's alterations, particularly after all Fiona had said to him earlier at the Kirk, in fact it caused Davie to give a wry smile.

CHAPTER 3.
A CALL TO BARRACKS.

Davie then recalled the day he went to the barracks of the Gordon Highlanders at Bridge of Don, just north of Aberdeen. There were quite a few rows of huts. Huts like the one he was entering which could accommodate sixteen men. The first things that struck Davie was how, firstly, young, and secondly, small, most of the recruited men were. That was, except for one chap who had taken up the bunk opposite Dave. He was tall, certainly as tall as himself, with a thick head of black hair. It was only about a minute later that the same chap walked across to Davie and introduced himself.

"Thomas Goodison folks call me Tam." He said, holding out a hand to shake, which Davie did as he told him his name. He told Davie he was from Dundee and the two soon sparked up a friendship.

The Spirit of St. Andrew

Davie leaned into Tam so's not to be heard by the others, "Jesus Tam, do you see the size of these lads, you'd think a good stiff breeze would blow them over."

"Yer right Davie......" replied Tam who then added, "......mind you I've heard a lot o' them have just enlister to get three square meals a day."

It was then the two were joined by another chap who it would turn out would be a constant friend all the way to France. He was small, around 5' 6", with bright ginger hair and had a strong Irish accent.

"William Copperweight, but I get called 'Ginger' all the time." He said as he shook the lad's hands.

"Is that an Irish accent Ginger?" asked Tam.

"It is.... He replied, "......moved to Dundee to work in the jute mills, then came to Aberdeen to get away from the smoke then had to put up with the stink of fish."

The lads laughed and would soon find out that Ginger would keep the whole hut going with his dry Irish humour.

Just then, a stocky looking character entered their hut and started to shout out at the men.

The Spirit of St. Andrew

"Right, you lot, my name is Sergeant McHarg and I'm here to knock you lot into shape so you can all go over to France and kick the shit out of Fritz!"

This caused all the men to give off a cheer, although they would soon find out that McHarg would put them through hell to get where he wanted them to be physically. As it turned out Davie and Tam would often find themselves having to help some of the younger, smaller lads in their billet. McHarg, with his gruff highland droll drove the men hard. One young lad, Billy McNeill, looked like he was in danger of losing his weekend pass one day at the bayonet practice.

McHarg had asked for a volunteer to go first and, stupidly or not, wee Billy stepped forward.

"My God......" went McHarg, "......all you bid hairy Scotsmen lined up and ye push forward a wee runt...."

Some of the men sniggered as McHarg continued, ".......oh, so some o' ye think this funny, well, laugh at this. If this wee bugger does not fully penetrate his bayonet into that jute sack down there, (He points to the row of hanging sacks) all them that thought it funny, will lose your weekend pass., and I know who you are."

All smiles were wiped from every face as they all looked to Billy, who, it had to be said did not look at all confident as McHarg approached him.

"Now Laddie......" he said as he pointed at the dummy, ".... that sack down there is not a sack....no no..... that, Laddie, is a dirty great German soldier who is about to shoot you through the balls......that is of course, if you have any......so, what the hell are you going to do about it?"

Billy quivered slightly before saying in a soft voice "Stab him Seargent."

"Then do it Laddie!" roared McHarg in young Billy's ear.

Billy took off as the men all looked on, hoping for the sake of their weekend pass that he would indeed puncture the jute bag. When Billy arrived at the sack puffing away, all he did was manage to push the sack into the air, unaware that it was fixed with a foot of loose rope at the bottom and if you didn't hit it with force, it just rose in the air.

"Get back here you pathetic excuse for a Gordon Highlander!" roared McHarg, "Now that you have lost your weekend pass, can we please have a man, step forward."

Billy had returned still panting and was first to speak, "Seargent...I'd like to try again please."

McHarg was brutal, "...get back in line you missed your cha....."

To McHarg's surprise some of the men interrupted, "......let him go again Sarg...." Yet others backed them, "....aye Sarg, give him a chance."

Without saying anything McHarg was pleased at the response, to him this was good comradery and he encouraged it as he held up a hand to stop the calling out.

"Very well, I'll let the wee bugger go again. But know this, if he fails again, you ALL, lose your weekend pass." Said McHarg with a wicked grin. Some of the men groaned at the prospect before they turned their attention to young Billy who was reading himself.

"Go on wee man, stick the bastard." Some shouted, before all the men caught on causing quite a roar to get up as Billy took off, fired by the men's shouting. Even McHarg joined in.

"Go on Laddie, you stick him, you stick him good!" He roared above all the men. Little knowing he would, from then on be known among the men as *"old stick 'im"*.

Billy himself let out the loudest roar, as he stuck his bayonet deep into the jute sack and twisted it with venom, before pulling it out.

Billy came back to a hero's welcome from the men, all pretty relieved that their weekend pass was safe. As well as McHarg being known now as *'old stick'im'*, young Billy would be known as *'bayonet Bill'* from then on. Several weeks passed and the men were ready to head south, firstly to Portsmouth, then on to France.

During all the time Davie was at Bridge of Don, young Wull was becoming quite close to Fiona as they went for their walks after the Kirk service.

Fiona had also still been seeing Alex Findley whom she had told of her plans with young William.

"You're becoming quite obsessed with the wee runt." said Alex, as Fiona arrived back from one of her walks with Wull.

Fiona picked up on his attitude, "......don't start Alex. I'm not in the mood."

Alex backed off somewhat, "Look Fiona I just want to know what you think you can gain from all of this?"

Fiona took a second to think, "What I want Alex is to get away from this bloody place and this bloody teaching job."

"Good grief......" answered Alex, ".... that's a few bloodies there......and I thought you like teaching."

Fiona looked skyward, "......please...... God, I hate every one of those little brats with their......please Miss this……and please Miss that. I just thank the Lord that I have a belt (*a leather strap for corporal punishment*) to shut them up."

"Jesus……." went Alex, as though a light had just gone on. "…. you're after their bloody farm to get yourself away from here!"

"Maybe." replied Fiona coyly.

"So….." continued Alex, now looking interested, "……just where the hell would you go?"

"Why the hell would you want to know Alex?" She demanded.

"Oh, I just thought you might want to go to America."

Fiona's eyes widened, "America……now that does sound good… but…" She said before her demeanor dropped, "how the hell would I get there with a war on?"

"As it happens……" said Alex, a large grin on his face, "……I know of a ship that goes there out of Glasgow. It takes a route down round the south Atlantic to avoid all the German submarines…. I could get tickets."

Fiona liked Alex idea, only problem was, would she want to go with him. He may be quite good between the sheets, if not a little rough, but she just felt she could never love the man and he may be hard to shake off.

Three weeks passed and once again Fiona found herself ready to go to the standing stones of Dyce with William Harley after the Kirk service. It was a sunny May Day and she seemed quite content with the idea. Fiona was finding that in a strange way young William was growing on her. Now that he had passed the over whelming gushing stage towards her, she found him rather good company. As it turned out there was a sad surprise waiting in the Kirkyard as Wull approached her. She could see his eyes were red rimmed as he uncontrollably fell into her arms.

"Jesus William what's wrong?" She demanded.

"It's my dad...." he said, "......he passed away last night."

Jim was found by Wulls mother Susan in the morning. He was sitting up in bed when Susan told him she would bring him up his breakfast. When she entered the bedroom Jim was sitting up in bed, his head slumped forward with his still lit pipe between his teeth. As Susan looked at him, she knew instantly that he was gone.

This of course meant the trip to the Standing Stones was off as Fiona returned home.

"So, old man Harley has gone..." said Alex coldly, after Fiona had told him of Jims passing.

"Jesus Alex you can be a right cold bastard when you like. James Harley was a good man." Snapped Fiona.

"Woe, seems I touched a nerve there. And here's me thinking that his passing was all part of your great scheme." Replied Alex.

"Perhaps......." replied Fiona defensively, "...but there's quite a few things would need to happen first".

Alex seemed to be enjoying the verbal jousting as he played along, ".... Let me see......" he said rubbing his chin with his hand and looking skyward, ".......Old man Harley's out of the way, the oldest brothers is off getting himself killed in France....so, that would mean the wee runt would be next up for the farm......" Alex then looked at Fiona with a wide grin, ".......by God Fiona you are good. This is all falling into place for us."

Fiona suddenly stared at Alex, "...us, what's this us, you're talking about?"

Alex seemed surprised by her tone, "......you and me.... off to America with the proceeds from the farm."

"In your dreams!" snapped back Fiona.

Her tone did not please Alex who, to Fiona's shock, suddenly grabbed Fiona by the throat.

"Now listen here Lady, I'm going out of my way to get these tickets to the States and I think that is your only way forward with this....so be nice!" He demanded.

"Get your fucking paws off me!" shouted Fiona as she brushed his hand away.

Alex backed off, "Sorry...." he said with a raised hand, "......I just want this all to work out for us."

Fiona stared into Alex, "I think you better get out of here...."

"Now why would I do that?" he demanded.

"Well, if you must know I've invited William round this afternoon and I think you should make yourself scarce."

Alex face twisted, "......but surely he'll be mourning with his family?" He quizzed.

"Of course, but I told him it may be better to have a quiet moment away with me to help him get through this." Said Fiona, hoping this would appease Alex.

Fiona looked on as Alex pondered on what she had just said, "......aye, that sounds like a good idea Fiona. It'll give you a chance to work on the wee runt."

The Spirit of St. Andrew

When Alex finally left, Fiona threw her back against the outside door in relief. She was now seeing Alex in his true light and knew he was becoming quite a problem that somehow; she was going to have to deal with.

Alex could only have been away five minutes when a knock came to Fiona's door. Fiona grizzled at the thought of Alex returning as she opened the door.

"What the hell do you........." she suddenly stopped and stared at Wull as he stood there slightly bemused by Fiona's demeanor.

"Oh William......." she said with a changed look of surprise, ".......do forgive me I thought you were

someone else. Please, do come in."

A rather downcast Wull entered Fiona's apartment for the first time, looking all around as he did.

"So......." asked Fiona, ".......to what do I owe this fine visit."

"Oh right......" said Wull, as he suddenly realised why he had called, ".......the undertaker just left the house as I got there. My dad's funeral is on Thursday......we....the family, were hoping you could attend?"

"But of course, William......" she replied, before patting the seat beside her on the settee, "......here, sit beside me William."

Wull sat down coyly beside her before he spoke, "actually Fiona, I wanted to talk to you anyway."

"Yes William, what is at?" Fiona asked.

"Well....I was wondering if you would be my steady girlfriend?" He blurted out.

Fiona smiled softly as inside she went...... got you!

She then decided to play along, "Well William......it is a bit sudden......." she said as she allowed a second for him to respond.

"Oh, I'm sorry Fiona I didn't mean to push you......." Wull didn't get to finish as Fiona suddenly lent forward and kissed Wull passionately on the lips, causing his eyes to widen before throwing his arms around her.

Poor wull was putty in her hands as she slowly moved the young man towards her bedroom.

Wull was in a rapturous daze as he let Fiona take control as they started to remove each other's clothing.

Wull suddenly stopped, "Fiona......."

"Yes......" She said softly.

"The thing is, I've never done this before......I'm sorry." He announced.

"William......" She said lustfully, "......just let it happen."And happen it did, for most of the afternoon, before Wull left floating on cloud nine.

As for Fiona, she was very pleasantly surprised by the young man's passion and lay on her bed caught in the arms of a dilemma. She had never in her live been treated so tenderly and passionately. Certainly not by Alex Findley nor any other man prior to that while studying in Edinburgh.

As for Wull, he danced and skipped all the way back to Drystanes and had to remind himself that he was supposed to be a young man in mourning.

The next Monday found Davie at the railway station of Aberdeen waiting to head south then on to France. As well as his mother there to see him off, there was his young brother and to Davie's surprise Fiona was alongside him. She was also saying goodbye to a young cousin who was also off to war. As Davie embraced his family before boarding the train, Fiona also closed in on Davie.

"Don't worry David...." she whispered in his ear as they embraced, "... I'll take care of William and the farm for you!"

Davie pushed Fiona away before being forced onto the train by the mass of men boarding, her words wringing in his ears.

What did she mean, 'Wull, and the farm'.

CHAPTER 4.
FRANCE.

Davie and his regiment of Gordon Highlanders had been marching through France for a couple of weeks now. The sound of artillery fire grew ever nearer as they marched along some French country road. Dailly, he had remembered Fiona's words to him on the station platform. It did little to ease his concern when he received letters from his mother stating how cozy Wull and Fiona had become together. Aside from the goings on at home Davie was enjoying the comradery of his fellow soldiers, in particular Tam and Ginger.

He remembered how earlier that day they all had filed past a farm house which had two rather large ferocious Alsatian dogs guarding the gate, they are held back by two chains. They were barking and snarling at all the men as they passed. Some in fact had to jump out of their way as they passed the dogs gnashing teeth. As well as the dogs there was a rather large French farmer who stood laughing at the men as they jumped out of the way of his two crazed looking dogs. Behind the farmer was a large garden area which was full of strawberry plants and lots of ripe berries.

The large farmer taunted the men as they passed, shouting in broken English, "Ha, no berries for ze eenglish today!"

To everyone's astonishment and surprise Ginger suddenly walked over towards the two crazed looking dogs.

"Ginger where the fuck are you going?" shouted Tam and others.

Astonishingly as Ginger approached with an outstretched hand, and to everyone's amazement the dogs seemed to calm right down and within seconds were licking Gingers hand and wagging their tails.

The big farmer was as shocked as the men as he tugged at the chains to real in the dogs away from Ginger. This caused all the men to cheer as the big farmer became more and more enraged.

The men spent the night in a field about a mile on from that farm and Davie was surprised when he woke early to find both Ginger and bayonet Bill were missing.

"Jesus Tam, ye don't suppose they deserted...do you?" asked Davie as the two stood scratching their heads. It was then that a couple of the other men came up to Davie and Tam and asked them if they'd seen their tin hats and water canteens, to which they were told they hadn't.

Suddenly it became clear what had happened when Ginger and Billy came sauntering in holding four tin hats full of fresh strawberries and canteens full of warm milk.

"Breakfast boys!" shouted Ginger, "The big fat farmer has made a kind donation to the war effort by supplying us with these goods".

".... but what about the dogs he had guarding the place?" asked one of the men.

"Och, they were like putty in Gingers hands." Said Billy.

"....and where did you get the bloody fresh milk?"

"Oh, I just decided to milk the fat bastards' cow as well......learned a lot on the farm when I was a kid." said Ginger, to everyone's amusement.

As well as Ginger keeping up the moral of the men Davie remembered that there were some down sides to things back then. He remembered the men, including himself, all staring into a field they passed which had hundreds of dead soldiers laying in lines. Davie did a quick tally and came up with four hundred dead and that was just one of many like fields.

Before long they were being filed into a trench. There were many soldiers already there and some of them looked battle-weary, thought Davie.

There were three trenches all around fifty yards apart. Davie and the lads were in the middle, or back-up trench, ready to support the front-line trench ahead of them. The third trench was where most of the supplies were held ready to be sent forward when necessary.

The first night in the trenches was a real eye opener. Explosions went off all around as earth and mud and God knows what else went flying into the air. Men could be heard screaming as they were hit with shrapnel and yet others blown to pieces. All the men knew it was down to sheer luck whether you took a direct hit. The barrage seemed to go on forever before the guns ceased in the morning. The men were told that usually meant an assault was coming on the front line and they would have to ready themselves in case the Germans took the front line before advancing on them.

Very little was said during this time as the full reality of just where they were hit home......it was, hell on earth.

Just as they thought it couldn't get any worse, it started to rain, and it poured down.

The Spirit of St. Andrew

Machine gun and rifle fire was ringing out from the front trench and beyond as Davie and the lads ready themselves for a possible attack if the forward trench fell.

"Jesus Davie......" said Tam loudly, "........if the Hun comes over the top here, we'll all be sliding about like ducks on a frozen pond!"

Davie just smiled at Tam and Said, "Well then, let's hope to God they don't."

As it turned out the front line held although there were many casualties, which is why the order to move up came through.

If Davie and the rest of his comrades thought they had seen some horrors before, it was nothing compared to what befell their eyes in the forward trench.

There were dead and injured lying about throughout the trench. Limbs and pieces of bodies were dotted around. The sound of the injured men's cries was the hardest thing to bear as those entering the trench felt helplessly unable to assist them. McHarg was roaring out orders to the men as to where they should go as they slipped about in the gutters caused by the still pouring rain.

"Try and dig a bit of cover for yourselves in the sides of the trench." Shouted McHarg.

Davie and Tam dug into an area big enough for them to crouch into, although it did little to stop the water from pouring over them.

Worse was to come slightly later that morning when the men came around with the big pot of stew for them to eat. It was watered down to less than a soup, although there were a few lumps of meat to chew on.

"Mmmm, delicious........" Said Tam sarcastically, "......wonder what's for dessert.... saturated semolina!"

As they moved into the night Davie decided to have a peep over the top of the trench. As he looked over all he saw was waist land. Thousands of creator hole and stumps of trees and tangles of barbed wire. The whole area was littered with dead and probably wounded men. About one hundred and fifty yards further on he could see the mound that told him it was the German trench.

McHarg then came around with instructions for the time ahead. "Right lads, were expecting Gerry to attack in the morning again and this should be preceded by a barrage from them tonight, so dig in and pray like fuck and make sure you're ready for him in the morning......let's give him a breakfast he wasnae expectin' lads!"

This brought a cheer from the men as Davie and Tam drew each other a concerned stare.

The Spirit of St. Andrew

As Davie sat with his knees up to his chest in a ball his thoughts wondered back home as he wondered how young Wull would be coping with the voluptuous Fiona.

As Fiona walked through the village one sunny afternoon in what was now late June, she happened to glance at the notice board outside the Police station which she often did as a matter of interest. She was taken by one particular notice which was headed, wanted for draft evasion, and was followed by a list of names. She got quite a shock when she saw the third name from the top was none other than Alex Findley. She was then taken by another notice on the board saying that an elderly lady, who had been badly beaten and left for dead, had been taken to hospital from her cottage to the north of the village, a Mrs. Hilda Findley. Police were on the lookout for a dark-haired man about 28 years old.

Both notices sent Fiona's mind racing as she thought to herself, my my, Mr Findley, you have been a busy boy!

As fate would have it, Fiona wasn't surprised to see Alex Findley waiting by her door as she arrived home.

"Well well......" she said coyly, as she opened her front door, "....... if it isn't the local draught dogger."

Alex twisted his face, "What the hell is that supposed to mean?" he demanded.

The Spirit of St. Andrew

"Don't come the innocent Alex, your name is on the Police notice board." Snapped Fiona, as she let him in.

"That......" he said, "......that, is a cousin o' mine, it's no me."

"Ah......" continued Fiona, "......would that be the same cousin who has assaulted your aunt in her cottage?"

Again, Alex twisted his face, "What the hell are you on about now Fiona?"

Fiona then turned to face Alex and stood arms folded, "Ok Alex, I'll play along, so if that is your supposed cousin on the notice board......why the hell aren't you in France fighting this war?"

"What? Do you think I'm mad, men are being slaughtered out there ninety to the dozen......anyway, I've a bad back.... I'm exempt!" he pleaded.

"Strange...." said Fiona quizzically, "......nothing much wrong with your back when you're bedding me."

"Ah well, you see Fiona that's the thing, a little exercise is good for a bad back." answered Alex with a sly grin.

Fiona changed tack, "Anyway, what are you doing here. If that is you on that billboard it means I'm harboring a fugitive."

The Spirit of St. Andrew

"Don't worry about that Fiona. The thing is I am here with good news...." he said invitingly.

"......and what would that be Alex?"

"Tickets to America...."

"What about them?" Asked Fiona.

"The boat sails every four months and the next sailing is in the beginning of August......" He said.

"August......but that's less than two months, I'll need more time than that. When is the next sailing after that?" She asked.

"Not until February next year."

This caused Fiona to slump into a chair, "Jesus......" she said dolefully, "......February, I'll never hold out till then."

Alex came over, put his hands on the arms of her chair and looked into her, "...then you'd better get to work on the wee runt!"

It was becoming quite a habit, Fiona and Wull walking out to the Standing Stones, and sure enough that Sunday saw them there once more. Fiona was working to get Wull on a hook as she started to quiz him.

"Do you love me, William?" she asked quietly.

"You know I do……" he answered, "……why do you ask?"

"Oh, it's just that I always dreamed that a handsome young man would take me away from this life that I live."

"You're not happy here?" Quizzed Wull.

"Oh, don't get me wrong William, I'm happy to have you……it's just this place…. teaching……I hate it all." she said.

"Jesus Fiona, I never realised that you were so unhappy……" he then did exactly what Fiona hoped he would when he suddenly went down on one knee, "…….Marry me Fiona and you can stay with me at Drystanes."

Fiona then bowed her head coyly, "Oh William that is so romantic but I just cannot see myself taking to the farm life. Could you see me feeding chickens and cooking meals all day?"

"Then we'll go away somewhere, somewhere you'll be happy……what do you think?" he asked pleadingly.

"I'm afraid William that the wages of a teacher don't stretch that far, and I have little savings." She said.

"You never know Fiona, one day I may own Drystanes and I could sell it off then we could set up somewhere." Said Wull.

"That's sweet William, but it could be years before that comes about."

"That's true, my fathers will is to be read this Wednesday and I know the farm will be left to Davie, but if he doesn't survive the war......then who knows." Said wull.

Fiona then frowned at Wull, "Really William you shouldn't think such things about your brother."

"I'm sorry......" he said, ".... I was just thinking out loud."

Fiona returned home that day with her mind all over the place. The thing that was surprising her more than anything was the fact that she was becoming very fond of young Wull, even though she knew someday, if everything was to pan out, she would have to desert him.

CHAPTER 5.
OVER THE TOP.

Five thirty in the morning and still it was raining. Davie and the rest of his regiment were on full alert after the nights bombardment from the Germans had finally let up. Only the occasional mortar exploded nearby. This told them that in all likelihood an assault on their trench was imminent. The men were then instructed to line themselves up along the trench in readiness for the attack.

Davie and Tam, being that bit bigger than the other men found the height of the trench just right for them leaning their riffle on and taking aim. The likes of Ginger and Bayonet Bill were having to find something to stand on to get comfortable with their stance. They both found a spot closed to Davie and Tam where a mound of earth had built up from mortar fire and men digging in. For a while an eerie silence fell over the place as everyone waited for the inevitable assault.

The Spirit of St. Andrew

Then, in the distance, the sound of roaring men could be heard. The attack was on its way.

"Hold your fire men......" Shouted McHarg, "......wait till they're about 100 yards away then open fire."

Tam turned to Davie, "How the hell are we supposed to know where 100 yards away is?"

"Not sure......" Answered Dave, "......but I could walk 100 yards in under thirty seconds, so we won't have long to wait mate!"

Just as the firing was about to begin the lads were taken by young Billy who had seen an old orange box which he thought would help his height on the trench. He had just gone about twenty yards from his post when a mortar shell exploded right beside him, killing him instantly.

His small body had been blown right up beside Davie, Tam and Ginger, as they looked and saw his head almost severed from his body. Ginger, who had become quite close to young Bayonet Bill was totally distraught as he went to his body. He knew there was nothing he could do but it only took seconds for his rage to overtake him.

Suddenly he grabbed his rifle and started shouting, "You fucking bastards......you fucking German bastards, I'll kill every last fucking one of you!"

The Spirit of St. Andrew

In Davie and Tams eyes, that was when all hell broke loose. Ginger climbed on to the top of the trench and on his knees, started shoot indiscriminately and erratically at all in front of him, still shouting out as he did so.

"Ginger get tae fuck down fae there you idiot!" Shouted Davie as Tam tried to pull him down.

Still, he fired and shouted, "……you bastards……"

That was when, to Davie and Tam's utter horror, a bullet ripped right through Gingers right eye and exited at the back of his head tacking part of his brain with it. It threw Ginger back into the floor of the trench where Tam jumped across to see what if anything he could do for Ginger.

"Ah Jesus, Ginger, what the hell have they done tae ye?"

Davie was still firing from the Trench with the German's getting ever nearer. That was when he heard McHarg shout at Tam.

"Goodison, get your fucking arse back on that trench right now!"

Davie on hearing McHarg went down

to Tam, "Hey big man, come on the Gerry's are right on top o' us."

"Auh Jesus Davie look what they've done to Billy and Ginger....we've got to get them help Davie." Said Tam not fully aware of the true state of his two dead comrades.

Again, McHarg roared, "Harley.....Goodison, get to fuck back up here now!"

Davie took a second to look into Tams eyes and they looked vacant as he stared at the two dead bodies.

That was it for Davie as he suddenly pulled at Tam, "Right Tam were out of here." said Davie, as he lifted Tam to his feet and helped over the other side of the trench from the fighting.

"Get back here you two......I'll have you up for desertion!" roared McHarg as Davie and Tam headed for the backup trench.

As soon as they got there a Captain in command of the backup trench shouted to some men, "Arrest those two men."

Before Davie and Tam knew it, they were being herded into a farm barn which the allies had taken over, the farmhouse itself was being used for their temporary headquarters.

The Spirit of St. Andrew

As Davie and Tam sat silently together along with half a dozen other men who had fled the scene. Davie turned his thoughts to home and what might be happening there.

It was a beautiful Sunday afternoon as Wull and Fiona returned from their usual Sunday stroll.

Fiona was grateful she entered her apartment first as Alex Findley was there waiting for her. Although she had told him to be away before she got back, it seemed he had defied her and stayed on. She quickly signaled to him to hide in the bedroom as Wull entered the house.

Wull was quick to put his arms around her and kiss her passionately. Fiona, although keen enough to kiss Wull, knew she couldn't encourage his passion at present. Not with Alex in the next room.

"Easy tiger......" she said with a smile, "......we've got all day."

"Sorry......" said Wull, as the two sat on the sofa together.

"So....." asked Fiona, ".... tell me about your fathers will?"

Wull hesitated as he drew Fiona a quizzical look.

"Oh goodness, I'm sorry William, that's none of my business." She said apologetically.

"No, it's ok, it's just as I expected, the farm will go to Davie when he gets back." Said Wull.

"....and heaven forbid that he doesn't get back?" probed Fiona coyly.

Again, Wull drew her a stare, "Then it'll go to me......"

Fiona's eyes widened, for she knew there was only a remote chance of Davie surviving the war. Sadly, for Fiona, his next words seemed to squash all her plans.

".......but not until I'm twenty-one......" Wull shook his head, "......would you believe it, my family think I'm not capable of running the farm until I'm twenty-one, I mean I do every job about the place I know the running of it inside out."

Fiona was just staring into space and was oblivious to all Wull's protestations, before she eventually snapped too.

"Oh, sorry William, I forgot my aunt Rose is visiting me this afternoon, you'll have to go." She ordered as she stood up to usher the startled youngster out.

Wull was taken by surprise, "When will I see you again Fiona?"

"I.... I'm not sure William, I'll be it touch." She said before closing the door on him.

"Well well......" said Alex, as he emerged from the bedroom. "......the best laid schemes, and all that......what now?"

"What now indeed." replied Fiona.

Davie spent a sleepless night in the French barn alongside his friend Tam. Mostly he just listened to the mumblings of the other men and the rain on the barn roof as it continued to pour down.

"Ah, yer awake Davie......" said Tam as he pulled himself up from the ground, "..........what do you think they'll do we us mate?"

"Not sure, but we'll find out soon enough."

Just as Davie said that, four soldiers came in through the barn door. One of them, a captain, ordered the lads to their feet before escorting them across to the farmhouse where they were brought before a group of three high ranking officers sitting behind a large desk.

The charge of "Deserting your post" was laid before Davie and Tam, who were then asked if they had anything to say?

"We saw our two best friends being killed and went to their aid and......." Davie was cut off by one of the officers.

"You know damned well that no matter what happens to your comrades you do not desert your post."

Again, Davie spoke, "It was my fault sir, I dragged my friend here over the trench because I saw he was distraught and I thought it better to live to fight another day, sir."

"Is that all, private?" Asked one of the officers, to which Davie nodded.

The three officers then whispered amongst themselves before one spoke.

"Right, we have decided you two are guilty of desertion. Now, not too long ago the sentence would have been death by firing squad, but his majesties government has put a stop to such punishments, so you two privates should consider yourselves most fortunate. Nonetheless, the sentence of this board is that you shall both be tied to the wheel of an active field gun for 72 hours with nothing but bread and water for nourishment........take them away."

Davie and Tam were surprised to see Seargent McHarg waiting for them outside.

"Right, you two......follow me." he ordered.

The Spirit of St. Andrew

"How are the rest of the lads sarg?" asked Tam as they set off.

"No thanks to you two, most survived, your friends McNeil and Copperweight and three others perished."

Soon they arrived at an area where there must have been at least twenty large artillery guns with large wheels which rock back and forth when fired. The first thing the lads saw was two other soldiers tied at either side of one of the guns and they did not look at all well. They were tied in the crucifix position, their legs barely reaching the ground causing them to dangle somewhat.

Davie and Tam were tied in the same position to the next gun up from the two lads. Still the rain fell as sometime later Davie and Tam watched as a group of men readied the gun for the next bombardment.

When the guns opened fire, for Davie and Tam it was like hell on earth, as they were thrown forward in a rolling motion then back in quick succession their arms nearly wrenched from their sockets as they battled in vain to get a foothold when they were thrown forward. The crescendo of noise as well soon had their ears wringing.

After about an hour it stopped, much to the lad's relief.

Davie, ears wringing, shouted out to his friend, "Are you alright Tam?"

"Aye...." came the reply, ".......but seventy-two hours of this may be a bit hard to take. How are the two lads on that other gun?"

Davie could only see one of them and he looked in quite bad shape as he battled to get a footing.

"They don't look too good." replied Davie, who circled his chin to try and relieve the wringing in his ears.

The still pouring rain was having a soothing effect on the lad's tied arms as they watched the artillery men ready the guns once more.

"Here we go again Davie." Shouted Tam.

Davie didn't heed Tam as he was taken by the approach of Seargent McHarg and the Captain who had held them when the crossed the trenches.

Davie couldn't believe it as he ordered the artillery men to cut Davie and Tam loose as well as the other lads on the other gun.

Barely able to stand they were brought in front of the captain and McHarg and given water to drink.

The captain looked at the men dolefully before he spoke.

The Spirit of St. Andrew

"I don't need to tell you men how bad the weather has been lately. The thing is we have been unable to send up spotter balloons or aircraft to see in what direction Gerry is moving. The balloons can't see through the low cloud and the aircraft Darrent fly that low for fear of being shot down. Now, this is where you chaps come in with a chance for your punishment to be rescinded."

Davie and Tam glanced at each other, glad to hear that from the captain, although they were both wondering what was coming next.

"We need some men to travel by foot across land towards the German lines, make a concise note as to which direction the bulk of the German forces and artillery are going, then report back to us."

The lads all looked at each other and could tell that they were all up for it, but the captain then gave they a sound warning.

"Now, you may all be thinking, no problem, but the thing is we know that Gerry will have machine gun nests dotted all over the place specifically to stop such a move by us. There is a very good chance you will all be picked of before you know what's happening. Now, the thing is I need to know here and now if you are to take up this task?"

The Spirit of St. Andrew

Davie and Tam knew by their uniforms that the other two lads were from English regiments. They were both young, no more that seventeen Davie reckoned and had been badly battered about by their punishment. Would they be any help to Davie and Tam if they took up this mission? Then again, thought Davie, if they are keen to go why leave the poor buggers to suffer, tied to those big guns?

After looking to each other, all four men nodded their approval to the captain. The captain then ordered McHarg to see to it that they were properly fed and kitted out for the mission.

As they were eating a very welcome breakfast of bacon sandwiches and coffee, the captain who told then his name was Forsyth, said that Davie would be in charge due to his knowledge of the land, he having worked a farm. He took Davie aside and showed him a map, pointing to a small hillock about two miles away. On the other side of that hillock Forsyth knew was a road the Germans were using to transport artillery and troops. Davie and the lads mission was to get details of just how much and in which direction these munitions were being moved.

Once ready the men were given back all their kit, including rifle and ammunition and were soon on their way.

The rain wasn't quite so persistent, down to a drizzle, though the sky was still very overcast.

"I'm Frank and this is James......" Said the tallest of the two lads, though he still just came up to Davie's shoulder, "......you're a couple of Scotch lads aint ye."

"No......" snapped Tam, "......we're a couple of SCOTS lads, SCOTCH is a drink....ye know, whisky!"

"Sorry......" replied Frank, "......no offence mate."

"None taken." Replied Tam with a wry smile.

"Are you two from London?" asked Davie.

"That's right mate, a couple of cockneys we are. Joined up at sixteen, lied about our age an all that." he said.

The men chatted amongst themselves as they made their way through some fields towards the raised area of ground Forsyth had told Davie about. They were approaching a good row of trees as Davie instructed the three others to quiet down.

Beyond the trees was a field which rose sharply. Davie ordered the lads to crouch down as he felt the top of this hillock would be an ideal place to set up a machine gun nest.

Just beyond the tree in front of them was a drystone dyke about three feet high. Davie told them to get in behind it as he surveyed the area trying to figure out what to do.

The Spirit of St. Andrew

"What now Jock?" whispered James.

Davie decided to ignore the Jock remark before he told them his plan.

He pointer threequarters up the hillock, "Do ye see the rise in the ground up there......like a molehill but bigger?"

"Clever buggers......." said Tam quietly, "......ideal place for a machine gun."

"Jesus......" said Frank, a hint of fear in his voice, "......if we go out there, they cut us to pieces.......what'll we do?"

"Ok, just keep calm...." said Davie reassuringly, "...... here's what we'll do. You see this dyke goes along and right up the side of the field......" they all nodded, "........you lads wait her while I head around the dyke and up in behind them."

The two Londoners grinned as they approved Davies plan.

"So...." asked Tam, ".......where do we come in?"

"I want you to give me a couple of minutes, then I want you to start shooting at them but keep yer heads down 'cos you don't have to be hitting them. Just draw their fire till I get in behind them." said Davie, causing them all to smile their approval.

Davie was off, crouched down behind the dyke. Soon he was heading up the side, praying he wouldn't be seen. Suddenly he stopped as he came to an opening where he figured a gate had once been.

"Shit!" he exclaimed, before whispering to himself, "......right lads I could do with a bit of distracting fire right now."

Davie couldn't wait and decided to go for it as he darted across the open space. He collapsed at the other side, overjoyed that he had made it.

Soon he was at the top and in behind the machine gun nest. He could see that it was manned by two men. It was then that Tam and the two lads opened fire.

The sound of the machine gun fire shot Davie right back to the trench a few days back. His hand shook as he fixed his bayonet to his rifle.

He figured he was about twenty yards back from the gun as he wondered how he was going to go about this.

Should he just try and pick the two men off from where he was. Yes, he thought, but what if I miss. This might give the two Germans a chance to turn the machine gun towards him......what then?

The Spirit of St. Andrew

No, he knew he had to move over the open land and get as close to them as he could without being spotted.

He then raised himself to a crouching position before he took off, holding his rifle out in the charge position.

Suddenly, when he was about halfway towards them one of Germens, the one feeding the machine gun, spotted him. As the German made for the pistol at his side Davie fired at him while still running. He saw the bullet ripe through the man's chest sending him back into the nest.

Davie could feel his heart pounding in his chest as his mouth went dry causing his breath to feel like fire on the back of his throat.

He fumbled franticly to at his rifle to engage another bullet as the other German tried desperately to turn the machine gun towards Dave.

As Davie ran, he suddenly heard in his mind Seargent McHarg bellowing out at him. *'You stick him Laddie...you stick him good, or he'll get you.... stick him'!*

As if obeying McHarg's order Davie drove his bayonet deep into the Germans chest, causing Davie to give out a roar. As he drew out his bayonet Davie saw the death throws on what he realised was a very young German's face.

He then gathered himself as he stood up and waved towards Tam and the two lads, all clear.

Davie then slumped down into the nest beside the two dead soldiers. As he looked, he saw one of them was wearing a wedding ring causing Davie to inhale deeply before bursting into tears.

"Jesus, God forgive me......what the hell have I done, these are just boys!"

Davie then pulled himself together as the others arrived.

"Wow mate, you did for them Propper an' no messing." Shouted Frank.

"Hae, let's see what they've got." Said James, as he jumped onto the nest and made for the two Germans pockets.

"You bloody well leave them alone!" Shouted Davie.

Frank wasn't for it, "Hae, spoils of war an' all that mate."

Davie then lowered his rifle towards them, "You get to fuck out of there now."

"All right...all right...." said the two lads as Tam turned towards Davie putting a hand on his rifle.

"Easy Dave......they're just daft boys." said Tam, causing Dave to come too.

"Right......" he ordered, "Tam, you come with me and we'll get the information we need for the captain......you two......ready that machine gun to take back with us."

Davie and Tam lay on the wet ground as they look at what was a massive movement of men and machinery all heading in a westward direction. They could see that something big was about to happen and it was all heading for an area Davie saw was called the Somme on the map the captain had given him.

Captain Forsyth was delighted with the information Davie had brought back.

"Well done you Men, this is brilliant work. You are excused your punishment and can now return to your regiments. Safe to say you will all be mentioned in dispatches.

Davie and Tam got a hero's welcome when they returned to the trench where the rest of the men were all getting ready to move.

"Any idea where were heading for Sarg?" asked Davie of McHarg.

"An area called the Somme." Replied McHarg dolefully.

Davie and Tam just drew each other a stare as they realised their destination.

It was early morning July 1st.

Davie and Tam were being ushered into a trench on the front line which was chock full of soldiers. Men were standing four deep and being made ready to go over the top.

The lads of the Gordon Highlanders had travelled through the night to get to the front line. They had seen the sky lit up with the bombardment the allies had inflicted on the German lines.

"Jesus......" said Tam to his friend, "......how the hell could anyone survive that?"

"You would think nobody could......but then again, these Germans are well dug in Tam." was Davie's

terse reply.

Around 6am the guns fell silent as word came down the line to prepare to attack.

Captain Forsyth was the officer giving the men of the Gordons their instruction.

"Right men, as you've all heard we have given Gerry a damned good pounding......" said Forsyth as a cheer got up, causing Forsyth to raise a halting hand, ".......alright settle. The order from high command is to just walk across no-mans-land, no running, and take over the German trench."
"Sounds simple enough Davie." Said Tam in Davies ear.

"Aye......" replied a rather dubious Davie, "......I'll believe it when I see it".

Whistles were being blown all down the line before arriving at Captain Forsyth who blew for the men to go. Davie and Tam were at the back row of the four as they waited for the men in front to head out over the top. The first thing that they heard which was worrying for the men was the sound of Germen machine gun fire.

"Jesus......" shouted Tam, ".......if Gerry is all blown to fuck, who the hell is firing those damned machine guns!"

When their turn came to go over, they remained together as they watched the men ahead of them being mown down by the machine guns. Morter's were going off all around them as well. As they made their way forward at walking pace as ordered, it became apparent to the lads that this was nothing short of a suicide mission. As they looked across at their comrades to their left, they could see a spray of machine gun fire making its way along the line towards them.

Suddenly as it was almost upon them Tam pulled Davie down into a crater hole just avoiding the volley of fire.

"Jesus fuck Tam but that was a near thing........" shouted Davie before continuing, "......what the fuck now?"

That was the second everything went black for Davie as a mortar shell exploded behind him.

Now sitting up on his hospital bed, he was able to recall all that happened on that fateful day. How crazy was it that the men were told to walk across no-mans-land. That's not to say they would have been any better running for the truth was that the bombardment by the allies had done nothing to dent the German forces, hence the slaughter on July 1st, 1916.

CHAPTER 6.
BAD NEWS.

Susan was busying herself over the kitchen sink when, through her window she saw a sight that's sent a shiver down her spine. The sight of a lone cyclist making his way up the farm road may, under normal circumstances, not have bother Susan but, this was a time of war, and everyone knew that telegrams were delivered by young lads on bicycles. It was a very sunny July morning as the young man handed Susan the telegram. It was bad enough that she had only recently lost her husband, but when she read that her son David had been killed in action, she literally collapsed down on to her knees.

Later, it was difficult for the rest of the family to console Susan as she mourned the loss of the two most important men in her life.

Fiona was in a foul mood as she heard a knock at her door. She had just got rid of Alex who had been demanding that he be allowed to stay at her place as the Police were all over his aunt's house.

"You should have thought more carefully before you assaulted the poor woman." She recalled telling him.

"I told you already Fiona that was my cousin.... not me." he retorted before leaving.

Convinced it was the returning Alex, Fiona opened the door ready with a sharp rebuttal.

"Look here......" was all she got out when she suddenly saw that it was Wull who was at her door. Wull ,with red rimmed eyes and a forlorn look which Fiona observed, just before she was about to send him on his way as well.

"Why William, whatever is the matter? she pleaded.

Fighting back tears Wull spluttered out, ".... it's Davie Fiona....he's been killed in action."

Fiona gasped as her hand went to her mouth, for as much as she had been rebuked by Davie, she still had a place in her heart for him.

"Oh my God you poor boy. Your family must be in tatters......please William, come in."

The Spirit of St. Andrew

As Wull entered Fiona's mind was in overdrive. What will this mean regarding the farm. Could it be closer to being young Williams, or will he still have to wait till he is 21.

"The telegram came yesterday......" said Wull, as he sat on Fion's settee, "......poor mums in a mess, there's just no consoling her."

Fiona sat down beside Wull and put a supporting arm around him as she wondered what to say to the grieving young man.

"Listen William, there was something I wanted to tell you and I know this will come hard for you but......" Fiona paused as Wull looked into her eyes, "......but I think I may be going away for a while......".

"What......." replied a very surprised Wull, as Fiona held up her hand to stop him.

"You know the school has come off for the summer and I feel the need to get away, so I might be away for several weeks." She said abruptly.

Wull looked, "But, you and me I thought......"

"That's the thing William, I'm afraid there won't be a you and me. You need to move on with your life. After all you'll have a farm to run in three years' time."

Wull thought for a moment then stood up to go, "I need to go Fiona, I've papers to attend to in Aberdeen."

Alex Findley was trying to keep as low a profile as possible. He was aware the Police were wanting to have words with him, and he knew why. That was why he was in Aberdeen; he thought the larger the crowd he mixed with the less conspicuous he would be. When he did visit Aberdeen, it was usually the harbour area he went to. He had gone out with fishing boats in the past, so he knew the harbour area. His connections there were the reason he knew about the ships going to America.

He was sat in the corner of the Harbour Bar having a pint when a familiar face entered the pub. A young man who he had seen at Fiona house, it was William Harley and he looked rather forlorn.

Wull stood at the bar as Alex approached him. Wull was having trouble with the barman who didn't seem to believe he was eighteen.

"It's ok Jim......" said Alex to the burly barman, "......I can vouch for him."

Wull stared at Alex, "......do I know you?" He enquired.

"Oh, you may have seen me around Dyce....I believe that's where you come from?" Said Alex knowingly.

"Right...." said Wull in a not too sure manner as he took a long swig at his pint.

"Wow, easy on son, you'll be pissed before you know it." said Alex with a smile.

"Who cares......" said Wull dolefully, as he then finished the rest of his pint, "......same again barman." as he turned to Alex, ".......and get my friend here one as well."

Alex then held out a hand to shake, "Alex Findley." He said, to which Wull shook his hand.

"Wull Harley." He replied.

"You don't look to happy Wull?" Quizzed Alex.

Wull thought for a moment, "You could say that Alex, after all I've recently just lost my father, my brother and the women I love doesn't want me."

"Wow..." went Alex, "......I can see how you're pissed off."

"Here's the thing though Alex, the women I love wanted to go away with me......you know......start a new life together. You see, when my father and brother died you would have thought I would be in line for my family's farm......right!"

The Spirit of St. Andrew

Alex was enjoying hearing young Wull unload his troubles and decided to coax him along, "Yes I suppose you would, so what's wrong?"

Wull finished his second pint, and with a slight scowl from the barman, ordered another.

"What's wrong Alex is in my fathers will, he said I would have to wait until I was 21 before I was able to get the farm, well, my girlfriend is not prepared to wait all that time......she said she couldn't work behind a kitchen sink and feed chickens and do all that farm work.......mind you I don't blame her, it's a shitty life for a woman."

"....and that's why she ditched you. That's tough luck Wull." said Alex, who was about to be surprised by Young Wulls next words.

"You're right Alex, that is tough luck, but here's the real chocker. My girlfriend.... or really, I should be saying ex-girlfriend, doesn't know there's another clause in my fathers will."

Wull stops to take another swig of his beer which is now starting to take effect on the young lad.

"Another clause Wull......" said Alex trying to bring out Wull.

The Spirit of St. Andrew

"Aye another clause that says if I get married before I'm 21, that I can take over the farm.......can you imagine that.....I mean what more will I know about a farm just because I happen to be married?" Said Wull, starting to slightly slur his words.

"Maybe they think you'll be more responsible or something. But surly if you tell your girlfriend about that she'll maybe marry you?" Said Alex, tugging at Wull again.

Wull then turned to Alex and waved a finger at him.

"No no, not on your nellie, do you think I want a woman just because she knows I'm about to come into a farm, plus the fact she'll think I'm just trying to get her because I now have a farm...." Wull then stared into Alex, "........she's a very perceptive woman is Fiona, and that's why I love her."

Alex could hardly believe his ears that all Fiona had been scheming for could now be well within her, or more to the point, their, grasp!

Alex couldn't wait to get back to Fiona and tell all about young Wull.

"What the hell are you doing here Alex, I told you I'm not for harbouring a fugitive." Said Fiona as she stood with her hand on her front door preventing Alex's entry.

"Oh well then....." said Alex coyly, "......you won't be wanting to hear the juicy news I've got."

Fiona cooled on hearing this, "News, what news?" She asked.

"News about another clause in old man Harleys will." he teased.

CHAPTER 7.
GOING HOME.

With the memories of the battle of the Somme now firmly entrenched in his mind Davie put thoughts towards going home as he dressed himself beside his ward bed. As he did, he was approached by a captain who was holding papers in his hand.

"Right Harley, the good news is that you are off home tomorrow......hopefully in time to prevent your own funeral since you asked us not to inform your family that you had not in fact been killed......oh yes, and I have a letter for you, I think it had been sent before your family received news of your demise Harley." Said Forsyth, as he handed Davie the envelope.

"Yes sir......right sir." was all Davie could think of to say after receiving such bad news.

As the captain left, Tam approached Davie, "So my friend that'll be the two of us off hame the morn.......canny wait to enter the Star and Garter in Dundee for a pint."

"Aye Tam, I might just join ye!"

The two chatted for a while before Tam left. Davie then opened the letter; it was from his mother Susan. Davie read with interest as she told him of Wulls romance with Fiona, which irked Davie. It further annoyed him when Susan told him she was sure Fiona was just after the farm, but she couldn't be one hundred percent certain, knowing the farm would pass to Davie. Jesus, thought Davie, if she thinks I'm dead, Fiona will probably be moving quickly to get things her way......time I was hame!

Fiona's mind was in overdrive as she listened to what Alex had said about Wull getting the farm if he were to marry.

"Jesus......" she cursed, "......and I've not long sent William on his way. So, let me think we have almost five weeks before the ship leaves for America."

"It's too tight Fiona......" said Alex, "......even if you get him to marry you, you need to show your bands at the Kirk for two weeks and even if he married you right away, that would only leave three

weeks to sell the bloody farm."

Fiona pondered Alex words, "That is true, but still possible, no reason why we can't get the wheels turning right away!" she said as she made to leave.

"Where the hell are you going?" demanded Alex.

"To see my future husband." Was her terse reply.

When Fiona arrived at the farm, she was pleased to see Wull outside working on a farm implement.

"Fiona......what a wonderful surprise what brings you out here?" He asked.

"To see you William......and to beg your forgiveness......" she said, bowing her head, even managing to force a tear from her eye.

"Forgiveness, whatever for......" He said as he pulled her in close.

"The way I've treated you. Only when you were gone did I realise just how much I loved you......and need you. Can you ever forgive me?" pleaded Fiona, her head now on his shoulder.

Wull put his hand on her chin and lifted her head before looking into her tear-filled eyes, "......you daft thing, there's nothing to forgive.......so, does this mean you'll still marry me?"

Suddenly Fiona's face lit up as she burst out, "......oh yes please William....as soon as possible."

"Right...." said Wull resourcefully, "......I'll put things in motion straight away."

"You will.......but......but......where shall we live?" Pleaded Fiona.

"Wherever the hell you wish Fiona." Said Wull excitedly.

"......but we'll have nothing to live on Willaim." said Fiona, goading Wull along.

That was when Wull informed Fiona about the other clause in his father's will.

"Listen Fiona, I didn't want to tell you this because I didn't want you marrying me for the farm, but there is another clause in my fathers will that says the farm can also be mine once I marry, even if it is before I am twenty-one."

Fiona played right along as she threw her arms around him and said, "Oh William that's the best news I've ever heard......so we can be together anywhere?"

"Yes, we can.... China, if you want!" shouted Wull.

"Oh William, I do love you." said a delighted Fiona.

The words were not long out of Fiona's mouth when see suddenly realized she did in fact love the young man.

The rate at which Wull and Fiona were moving things quite staggered Susan and Cathy. No matter how hard they tried to tell Wull to take time, think things through properly. They even risked Wull walking out when they said it could be the case that Fiona was using him for her own ends. The thing was Wull was so head over heels in love, nothing they could say was going to deter him. What truly shocked them was when he told them that he wanted the farm signed over to him before he married so he could set the wheels in motion.

"Don't worry......" he told them, "........when I sell it, I'll make sure you get to keep your houses......that's only fair."

To Wulls mind he was being more than fair, after all he was still ranking from being made to wait until he was 21 originally. The "being married" clause eased his hurt somewhat, especially now he was to marry Fiona.

"So...." said Alex, as he leaned against the sink in Fiona's living area, "…….. you've got your joint bank account we the wee runt."

"His name's William, and yes you could say we are good to go."

"……and you've transferred all your pennies into the account?" asked Alex, quite sure that she hadn't.

"Don't be ridiculous Alex my money is all put aside for leaving for America in three weeks."

"Jesus three weeks. That's cutting things a bit fine when you're to be married in a few days."

"No need to fret Alex, my William already has a buyer all lined up. It seems there's a neighbouring farmer has been after their farm for years……it's all good to go." said Fiona rather glibly.

"…. of course, Ian McGill, he's been buying up everything in the area lately." Said Alex knowingly.

"Yes……now Mr Findley I need you to go……." said Fiona as she handed him his jacket.

"Why……where the hell are you going?"

"To the service in the Kirk, a remembrance service for David Harley." She told him.

"Of course, the late Davie Harley……didn't you have a thing for him as well?" He teased at Fiona.

Fiona drew Alex a rather blank stare, "Just go Alex….please."

The Spirit of St. Andrew

CHAPTER 8.
THE WEDDING.

Fiona was scurrying about getting herself ready for her big day. Her main annoyance was the presence of Alex Findley who was just making a complete nuisance of himself.

"Are you not being a bit cheeky getting married in white?" he taunted.

Fiona snapped, "For God's sake Alex why don't you just fuck off and leave me to get ready. My Uncle will be here with his car any minute."

Fiona was being taken to the Kirk by her uncle, his daughter Alice, Fiona's cousin, being her bridesmaid.

Wull had booked them into a hotel in Aberdeen for their honeymoon after a reception at the farm.

Alex continued to annoy Fiona as he said, ".... now is that any way to talk to the man who has something very special for us."

"Alex, I'm not in the mood for your taunting.... what is it?" Alex then drew from his jacket pocket two boarding tickets for the boat to America.

"Well, at last something useful from Alex Findley." Said Faina sarcastically.

"Indeed Fiona, and I'll just hold on to them until it's time to leave in a couple of weeks." He said, as he slipped them into his inside jacket pocket.

Right up to the last-minute Susan was trying to pursued her son not to go through with the wedding.

"Listen mum, I know you mean well, but me and Fiona will be great the gether you wait and see." reassured Wull, as he slipped on his best suit jacket.

Wull and Jack, his best man, were waiting for the taxi that would take them to the Kirk.

The Harley family arrived at the Kirk in plenty of time as Wull fussed about, getting everyone seated, as they awaited the arrival of the bridal party.

The Spirit of St. Andrew

Around this time a train drew in to Dyce station. It was the 1:45pm from Aberdeen and was on time. A Tall soldier dressed in a Gordon Highlander uniform alighted the train.

It was Davie Harley, home from the war. He was surprised as to how few people were going about as he remembered Dyce being a busy station on a Saturday afternoon.

As he left the station, he met a friend of his from his footballing days, it was Jim McIntyre, a little chap who played on the wing, he, although small, was built for speed, that being his asset on the field.

As he faced Davie he took a backward step, ".... Jesus, Davie Harley, we were telt you were deed!"

"Aye...." replied Davie, "......I thought you might......where the hell is everybody?"

"What? ye dinny ken, they're all at yer brother's wedding in the Kirk, kicks off at two o'clock."

Rain started to fall as Davie glanced up at the station clock which he knew was always at the right time...... "1:50pm...." He mumbled, ".... Beter get my arse down there then Jim."

As Davie approached the entrance to the Kirk yard a small Morris car crept past him. As he looked into the car, he saw an astonished looking bride staring back at him.

By the time the car arrived at the entrance to the Kirk Davie was alongside it. Fiona's uncle got out of the car and came around to open the door for the bride to alight.

As this was happening one of the ushers at the Kirk entrance was so astonished at seeing Davie Harley he rushed into the Kirk and quickly sat down beside Wull and Jack on the front pew.

In as loud a whisper as he dared, he spluttered out at Wull, "Wull, yer no goin' tae believe this but your brother is outside the Kirk......he's alive Wull, he's alive!"

This of course was overheard by most people inside the Kirk as Wull got up to go. Astonished conversation broke out as everyone started to rise and go outside.

As Fiona stepped from the car her bridesmaid opened an umbrella to shelter her from the now heavy rain. Fiona staggered slightly as her eyes met Davies.

"Jesus David, you're alive.... thank God!" She said, a slight look of alarm on her face, as she went on, "......you should go into the Kirk, the service is about to......."

Suddenly Davie cut her off, "……. there'll be no service Fiona." Said Davie just as an astonished Wull came running on the scene. He immediately embraced his brother.

"Davie, my God it really is you, how the hell……." Davie cut in on his younger brother.

"I'll explain it all later Wull, though I don't think you'll be too pleased to see me when I tell you what I have to say."

Wull stopped momentarily, looking at Fiona first and then to Davie.

"What the hell's going on?" He snapped.

"I've no idea William, perhaps your resurrected brother will enlighten us." Said Fiona as she looked towards Davie.

"She's only marrying you for the farm Wull." Davie blurted out.

"What the hell are you talking about David. That is just rubbish." Said Fiona as she looked pleadingly towards Wull.

Davie held up his hands to stop anyone else speaking, "Right……" he demanded, "…. I am back to claim the farm as is my right, so with that Fiona, are you still going to marry Wull today?"

Everyone went silent and unfortunately it was too long a silence for Wull as he stared into Fiona's eyes.

"Jesus Fiona……..he's right, isn't he……." said a dumfounded Wull.

"William of course this does change thing ……..maybe I just need a while to…….." Fiona didn't get to finish as Wull set off through the rain back towards Drystanes farm.

Davie looked deep into Fiona's eyes which were either tear filled or affected by the rain as what seemed like tears running down her face.

As other members of Davies family then clamoured around him patting him on the back while him mother embraced him, Fiona instructed her uncle to take her back to her home. The wedding was most definitely off.

Back at her house Fiona was in a daze as she thought over all that had just transpired. She most certainly was not in any mood for Alex Findley.

"Dear o' dear……." said Alex as he emerged from the bedroom, "……..that was either one hell-of-a-quick wedding, or you are still a single woman."

Fiona was in no mood for Alex as she turned away from him and said, "I thought I told you to fuck off Alex......and you're right, there was no wedding."

"Now just you hold on there missy, I have tickets for America here and wedding or no wedding I need cash to get to hell out of here because I've just found out that my dear old aunty has died from her wounds." He said, his voice raising as he spoke.

Fiona, standing with her back against her sink, gave a wry smile as she said, "......and why should that worry you Alex, I thought it was your, unknown cousin, who attacked the poor woman."

"Never mind all that...." He went on, "......the thing is there's no money from any farm sale......so.....?"

"So, what......Alex?" Snapped Fiona.

"So.....I do believe you told me you emptied your bank account in readiness for putting it into you and the little runts joint account. I'm afraid I need that money.... now!" He demanded.

"Over my dead body!" retorted Fiona sharply.

"Oh, that can easily be arranged." Shouted Alex as he lounged at Fiona, grabbing her by the throat and causing Fiona to scream.

The Spirit of St. Andrew

As Alex squeezed at Fionas neck she started making a choking noise as he pressed her body against the sink. Fiona was feeling the life drain from her as she suddenly managed to muster enough energy to bring her knee up sharply into Alex groin.

This resulted in Alex realising his grip enough for Fiona to bring both her arms up quickly, releasing Alex grip.

"You fucking bitch!" He shouted as he staggered back a couple of feet.

As he did, Fiona knew he wasn't finished his assault on her as she felt around the worktop beside her kitchen sink for something to defend herself with.

As she watched, Alex prepares to attack her once more, she felt a vegetable knife she had been using the day previous.

As he lounged forward Fiona held the sharp knife out towards him. Alex's own momentum drove him on to the knife which pierced under his ribcage and into his heart.

Alex's eyes bulged as he looked into Fiona's astonished face. Fiona knew he was dead before he slumped to the ground.

The Spirit of St. Andrew

"Oh my God what the hell have I done." Shouted Fiona out loud, as she then bent down and slapped Alex's cheek, just to make sure.

Fiona then slumped into one of the kitchen chairs beside her in an effort to gather her entangled thoughts.

I've murdered a murderer, surely, they won't prosecute me for that, and it was self-defense. Were her first thoughts.

Again, she considered, even though, they'll still arrest me, throw me in the cells……to hell with that! I'm out of here!

Next thing she knew she was rummaging through Alex pockets. First, she found the tickets for America and then, to her surprise twelve pounds in one-pound notes. Poor Mrs. Findley's life savings no doubt, she pondered. Fiona then went to her sideboard drawer and took out the money she had withdrawn from the bank from her own account. She counted, ninety-two pounds.

Right, she said out loud, "That'll get me a start in the states".

Fiona was thinking on her feet, she was sensible enough to know that they would find Alex's body fairly quickly and she would be the prime suspect. With that, she realised she would never get past any customs or port authorities as Fiona Thompson.

The Spirit of St. Andrew

She was well aware that passports were now required when leaving the country and suddenly remembered that she and her sister Jean took out passports when they went to Paris just after Jean married to celebrate Fiona qualifying as a teacher.

"Somewhere here......" she said as she felt to the back of the drawer. Sure, enough she still had her and Jeans passports.

How fortunate I look so like my late sister, thought Fiona, as she looked at her sister's passport.

Fiona glanced at the clock on her wall, 2-45pm.

Good, there's a train to Aberdeen at 3-10pm, I should make that, she thought, as she then started to pack a suitcase.

As she left the house wrapped in a shall which was covering her head, she was delighted that the rain was pouring down, causing everyone to stay indoors.

As she boarded the train, she knew she would have to spend nearly two weeks hiding in Glasgow before the ship set sail. As it would turn out she found the seediest little hotel available and just lay low.

Boarding the ship was no problem as she was now Jean Harley, and no one questioned her about her passport.

The Spirit of St. Andrew

At Drystanes farm after the wedding, Wull spent most of his time in his room, that was until a couple of days later when the Police came calling.

Wull was called down to the kitchen area where he sat and took in what the Police were saying.

There was one uniformed officer and one detective, a sergeant Brown from Aberdeen.

"We have reason to believe that you are......em sorry, were the fiancé of one Fiona Thompson......is that correct."

Wull just nodded.

"And have you any idea as to her whereabouts Sir?"

Wull didn't answer directly, "Why......what's wrong?" He queried.

The officer didn't answer, rather he pulled a photograph from his inside jacket pocket and held it out in front of Wull.

"....do you know this man Mr Harley?" He asked.

Wull looked at the picture which was of Alex Findley, no doubt got from his aunt's house.

Wulls eyes widened as he recognised the man who spoke to him in the Harbour Bar in Aberdeen.

"Yes......" said Wull, ".......I had a drink with him in a pub in Aberdeen about a month ago......why?"

"Well, Mr Harley, this man's body was found in Fiona Thompsons house stabbed through the heart."

"Oh my God!" Exclaimed Susan, who was listening in and then said, "......and Fiona......where is she......did she do it?"

The Police officer held up a stopping hand.

"Hold on Madam were not at liberty to disclose any information about the case other than we are looking for Miss Thompson who appears to have gone on the run. So, I'll ask you again Mr Harley, have you any idea of her whereabouts?"

"I've told you already.... no." Answered Wull dolefully.

As Wull returned to his room he was able to build a picture and it didn't make for good reading. He remembered telling Alex about his father's will and he now realised that the man in that photograph then passed on this information to Fiona. Wull now realised he had been dupped and that Davie and the rest of the family were right about Fiona only wanting the proceeds from the farm. Fiona of course was never found by the Police.

It wasn't long after, that Wull who had gone into Aberdeen just as Davie had done, came home to announce that he had enlisted. This of course horrified Susan although she was slightly appeased when she heard it was the catering corps he had enlisted into.

Davie reassured Susan that he would be nowhere near the front line.

It also turned out that Davie did sell the farm to Ian McGill on the understanding that he leased it back to Cathy and Jack to run and that the farm house was to be no part of the deal and would remain within the family.

Davie was soon contacted by his friend from the trenches Tam Goodison who told Davie he was off to sea with the merchant navy and wondered if he was up to joining him. Davie knew there was not enough work for him at the farm and knew he could never be stuck in some factory working for what he knew would be poor wages.

After he had made arrangements with his sister Cathy to look after his son and daughter while he was at sea, he decided to set off with his good friend at the end of the war.

After the war ended, Wull was only home about two weeks when he received a letter from America which he took to his room to read, it was from Fiona.

The Spirit of St. Andrew

Dear William,

Now that this damned war is over and I hope you survived that great ordeal, I thought I would get in touch to put a proposition to you.

Perhaps by now this letter is already in the back of your fire and I wouldn't blame you if it was.

If not, I would like to say how dreadfully sorry I am for the way I treated you, but you must understand William that despite all that happened I found that I just could not put you out of my mind.

When I defended myself against Alex Findley, I knew it would be hard to explain to the authorities what happened and I had to flee.

I have set up in business here in America and could do with a good worker to help me. I have a small tobacconist shop here in Boston and am looking to expand. Please believe me when I tell you that I still love you and will wait for you for six months, if by then you are not here, I will fully understand and move on with my life and leave you to yours.

Yours in anticipation, Fiona.

Within two months, Wull was away.

CHAPTER 9.
SHORE LEAVE.

The "Empress of The Clyde", an 11,000-ton merchant ship dropped anchor in Savanta harbour on a balmy August afternoon in 1936. She was a large merchant ship from Scotland, its cargo, mainly scotch whisky, with the purpose of returning to Britain with coffee beans and bananas. She had been at sea for three weeks, skirting the coast of Africa before heading for South America. Savanta was the capitol of Bavaria, a small republic just north of Brazil, run by a dictator named Phillipe Ramon, a man who was fashioning himself on the fast-growing Adolf Hitler in Germany. Fast growing of course in power, he had already annexed Austria and had his sights now set on Czechoslovakia and who knows what other European countries thereafter.

Phillipe Ramon in comparison was very small fry, though this hadn't prevented him from making life very difficult for those living under his regime. Anyone opposing his ideas was quickly made to disappear, just as Hitler had done during the night of the long knives. He had also adopted the swastika flag and had them draped from many of the city buildings. He had already built a small army but didn't have the financial clout to go much further and could only beg so much from Herr Hitler.

Because of this dictatorial stance, he had forced other countries to break of any alliances he had with them, mostly due to the way he was treating his people. Britain was what you would call "border line tolerant". Hence the reason the "Empress of the Clyde" was still able to deal with this country.

The ship's captain was a tall, dark bearded Scotsman named Gordon McLean who had fifteen years of service under his belt. He did not like stopping over in Savanta though. He found it a very unpleasant place and could see the troubles the people were having to bear first-hand whenever he stepped ashore. Sex workers were very prevalent along the quayside, looking for fun seeking sailors who had shore-leave money to burn and had plenty of pent-up frustrations in need of satisfying. The people in general looked hungry and the captain could see plenty of beggars as he walked the streets.

He just could not agree with what was happening in Savanta and his mind set was, get the job done and get to hell out of there.

As it was, two of his crew were quite happy to go ashore, Tam Goodison and Davie Harley. The two lads now in their late thirties who had served in the merchant navy for more than 15 years. They had made their friendship while serving as young men in the first world war and saw action together in the Somme where both men had been badly wounded. Tam and Davie had both recovered in the military hospital together where they traded stories and developed a bond that would see them follow each other into the merchant life a year after the war.

They had both remained bachelors but Tam was happy to boast a girl in every port and there had been many ports. By "girl", he probably meant prostitute. He still stood tall with a solid build and a crop of dark brown hair. He had a four-inch-long scar running from his hairline down to below his ear on the right side of his head, the result of a close encounter with a German bayonet. Although away from home most of his life he still held on to his strong Dundonian accent. He was quite proud of his roots and still, when possible, looked out for the results of Dundee football club.

"Ah, dinnae worry Davie," He'd gibe at his friend, "Yer shitty Dons (Aberdeen Football Club) are in for a hidin' fae the Dee this weekend."

To which Davie, who had remained his friend during the best part of 16 years in the merchant service said to Tam to stop his 'dreaming'.

Davie was content to know the farm he owned for only a couple of weeks was being well looked after by his sister Cathy and her man Jack who were also responsible for bringing up Davies two children while he was at sea.

The Spirit of St. Andrew

When home from the sea he would stay with his daughter who had her own house in the city of Aberdeen.

The sea life was a great escape for both men, they had both thought about shore jobs early on after the war but the mundane feeling of seven thirty to five thirty was just too entrapping. Davie's brother Wull, was now settled in America, and Davie had thought long about going out and joining him when the war ended, but the work his brother offered seemed little different from jobs he could get at home.

Both Davie and Tam had struggled after the horrors of the Great War. They had seen things that no man should have had to endure. Bodies blown to pieces right in front of their eyes. Men mown down by machine gun fire, sometimes cutting their bodies near in half. Men, still alive, holding their guts in their hands and screaming for help, Tam, in one instance, shooting a screaming British soldier through the head to relieve his agony, though that was never spoken about.

It was a relief for both men to find the merchant navy and let them get away from city life. Too often, to easily, men would make a jibe about the war that would set them of on the defensive. Before they knew it, they would be rolling across a pub floor fighting over something trivial, something that, had it not been for the War, they would never have entertained.

Most of the rest of the crew on the ship were Scots as well, though Tam and Davie stuck together when going ashore. They had been to Savanta before and were none to impressed with the set up there.

As they readied themselves for shore leave, they discussed their previous visit to the city.

"How many different cities do you think we've been to Davie?" Asked Tam as he folded at his shirt collar.

"Jesus Tam, now you're askin'……. More than twenty, I'd think……why d'you ask?"

"Well, I was just thinkin', did ye ever visit one as shity as Savanta?"

"No Tam never, but it still won't stop you fae hankering' after it's ladies o' the night".

Tam grinned, "That's true big man, but ye canae blame the state o' the city on the poor bloody women now, can ye?"

"Aye well," replied Davie, "you just remember tae use a Frenchie (*Condom*) when ye do have a pop at one o' them."

"Always Davie always………here, Davie, do you remember the Frenchie they issued us we durin' the War?" Asked Tam we a snigger.

"Jesus' aye, as thick as a wellie boot and, reusable." Replied Davie.

"That's right. Do you know this Davie, I had that Jonny for ten years after the War."

The Spirit of St. Andrew

"Augh yer jokin' Tam…….ten years? God ah hope ye wash it out every time ye used it."

"Dinnae be daft, ah just wiped it along the carpet……."

"What! Ye clarty bastard." Shouted Davie.

Tam laughed, "Ye daft bugger, of course ah washed the damned thing, what kind o' a midden do you think ah am."

"Nothin' would surprise me Tam. Anyway, ah hope yer well-armed the night, or have ye still got the one fae the War?"

"Very funny, ah telt ye ah only had it for ten years…. served me well though." Said Tam as they made to leave their cabin for shore.

On deck captain McLean was waiting to address the men before going ashore.

"Right lads, best behaviour the night, this is a rough place, thugs and crooks on every corner. Remember to stay in two's at least and don't go to deep into the city. The women are horny…. (This caused the men to cheer) ……alright, calm down. Yes, their horny, but there dangerous as well, they'll pass on diseases and steal your wallet as quick as blink an eye……so, ca canny boys, ca canny."

It was early evening as Davie and Tam hit the skirts of the town just back from the harbour dressed in white shirt and dark flannels, they felt quite dapper. Sure enough, there were women on most of the street corners waving the lads toward them.

"Jesus Davie, look at that we beauty there, she's screamin' for it, Ah'd love a rattle at that."

Davie put his hand on Tam's shoulder, "Easy Thomas, easy, it's early yet, come on, let's find that bar we were in the last time we were here. Ah seem tae remember winin' a few pounds at the poker table."

Tam was still ogling the young woman, "You're mad Davie, ah mean, how could ye put gamblin' before a good lookin' dame?"

"Put it this way Tam, am no likely tae get a dose o' the pox playin' cairds, in fact, ah might just win a few bob."

Tam reneged and walked away from the still beckoning prostitute. They soon arrived at the bar. The name above the door was in Spanish but the lads recognised it from their last visit, it was the "Blue Dragon". Inside, it was quite full and heavy with smoke from the cigarettes and cigars that were smoked by most patrons.

Tam ordered two beers from the bar as Davie looked around for a vacant seat at one of the several card tables that were available. The place reminded Davie of one of the bars he had seen in westerns shown at the picture houses in Aberdeen. Only difference was that most of the men here were dressed in white as opposed to cowboy gear from the movies. Most seats were taken, though

Davie spotted one near the back against the wall and nodded at Tam to follow him.

Four other men were seated at the table. The one with his back to the wall was well dressed and had a look of importance about him. He was smoking a half-finished cigar which he held between his teeth most of the time. When he grinned it showed up his yellow teeth of which one incisor was gold. The dealer sat next to him on his right, a rather large sweaty chap who looked uncomfortable dealing. The other two looked more like common peasants who were maybe trying to get a boost towards their meagre income.

Davie looked at the cash in front of the men and there was little doubt the yellow toothed man was doing the winning. There were a few people around the table watching and it surprised Davie that there was a vacant seat, but he sat on it anyway.

"Ah! A sailor I think, yes?" Asked the well-dressed man.

"That's right." Replied Davie, before continuing, "You speak English?"

"Si," Replied the man, "Well a little." He then went on, "You are English, yes?"

"Scottish, actually." Replied Davie.

"Ah!" Said the well-dressed man, "Scottish, then you are like us, you hate the English as well, no!" This caused a

The Spirit of St. Andrew

slight ripple of laughter amongst the patrons who understood him.

"No, not really." Replied Davie, who then changed the subject, "So, it's five card poker then?"

"Si, and no limits." Was the reply.

Davie took money from his pocket that he had been given by Captain McLean for shore leave and placed it on the table. Tam was standing behind Davie watching the play.

First thing Davie noticed was how clumsy and slow the dealer was and it made him feel uncomfortable, but he said nothing. To his slight surprise Davie won the first hand. A small pot, but a win none the less. You would think winning straight away would please Davie, but he'd been around games long enough to know a set-up when he sees one. You lull the sucker in with a few wins before cleaning him out.

The well-dressed man won the next two hands causing one of the two peasants to storm back from the table cursing his luck as he went.

"Ah, a bad looser I think." Said the man, with a large yellow smile.

Davie was now becoming suspicious of the well-dressed man. Why did he flick the ash from his cigar under the table when there was a large ash tray in front of him? Something wasn't right!

The Spirit of St. Andrew

Next game there was quite a pot building. Davie had two pairs and was confident. Once again, the man flicked his cigar below the table, Davie called as he did. The yellow toothed man grinned broadly as he turned over four kings. Davie threw in his cards and the man reached out with both hands to scoop the pot. Suddenly, before he could draw the money away Davie grabbed him by the wrists and squeezed.

"Augh!" The man yelled, "what are you doing signor?"

"Stand up!" Demanded Davie, as a silence fell over the place.

"What?" Shouted the man.

"Stand-to-fuck-up." Davie squeezed harder.

Suddenly the dealer made to grab at Davie, but Tam pushed him back.

"Si! Si!" Said the man who slowly rose from his seat. As he did to everyone astonishment two playing cards fell from his lap. A gasp went around the onlookers who all instantly realised that the well-dressed mas was indeed cheating.

"You cheatin' bastard!" Shouted Davie who then handed out the standard punishment for anyone caught cheating at cards, at least where Davie came from, as he punched the man square on the jaw. As the man fell backwards against the wall, to Davies surprise a large cheer went up from those around the table. It seemed that this was not a popular character amongst the locals, and they enjoyed seeing the appropriate punishment being dished out.

Sadly, the incident didn't end there as suddenly the big dealer pulled a stiletto flick knife from his waist and made to lounge at Davie. Quick as a flash Tam saw this coming and lifted the card table upwards in time to see the knife stick in the table about half an inch from the top and a couple of inches from Davies stomach. Wide eyed Davie and Tams stare met, before Tam then swung around and dished out the same medicine to the fat dealer as Davie had to the well-dressed man.

Yet another cheer went up from the crowd. As they cheered the two peasants who had been losing in the game quickly picked up Davies winnings from the floor and handed it over. Once again, the onlookers were delighted to see Davie give the two men a small amount of his winnings which Davie knew they had been cheated out of. While all this was going on Tam had taken a shine to the stiletto flick knife which was still sticking out of the half-upturned table. Quick as a flash he grabbed it, quickly folded it, and slipped into his pocket.

Davie and Tam made to leave with people slapping them on the back as they went, giving further reassurance to Davie that the well-dressed man was not a popular character. As they arrived at the door Davie turned in time to see the two peasants escorting the yellow toothed man and the dealer out of the back door, Davie giving a wry smile as they went. As he left, he and Tam discussed how the man was cheating by having the poor dealer slip him one or two extra cards during each game. The ones he didn't need he then very discretely dropped on to his lap, before retrieving them at the end of the game when he went to flick the ash from his cigar. "Right Mr Harley," proclaimed Tam, "Allow me to escort you to the next pub and help you spend your winnings on some fine booze and exotic ladies".

CHAPTER 10.
MURDER.

The following morning Davie and Tam were wakened from their drunken sleep by some loud banging on their cabin door.

"What the fuck!" Exclaimed Tam, as he raised his thumping head from the pillow. "Davie…. Davie, are you hearin' that?"

" Aye, tell whoever it is tae fuck off!"

Before Tam could do that, a voice sprang from the other side of the door, "You two are wanted in the captain's quarters Immediately."

"O' Jesus Tam what the fuck did you do last night we that ugly tart I saw you take off we?" Demanded Davie, his face contorted by hangover pain.

"Excuse me she was not ugly, and I definitely feel a sense of jealousy in your tone Davie boy."

Davie slid from his bunk, "Don't make me laugh, she even had a glass eye, not to mention a towsy old wig…....aye and nae tits either."

"Aye well, you don't look at the mantlepiece when yer pokin' the fire." Was Tam's terse reply as he opened the door to leave.

A rather scary surprise awaited the two lads as they approached the captains quarters. Two local Policemen were standing at the doorway, and they could see what looked like another, more senior officer, inside with Captain McNeil.

"Jesus Tam, what the hell did we do last night." Said Davie, as the two arrived and went in, followed by the two constables.

"You wanted to see us Captain?" Asked Tam.

"Yes Lads….em… this is Inspector Gonzalez of the local constabulary. He speaks English so I'll let him explain……" said Captain McLean, holding out a hand towards the Inspector.

Inspector Gonzalez was a tall good-looking man about the age of fifty with the usual black moustache customary to the area and looked particularly smart in his dark blue uniform.

"Right gentlemen, I'll get straight to the point. I'm here to arrest you both for the murder of one Jose Ramirez. Mr Ramirez was found dead behind the premises of the Blue

Dragon cassino in the early hours of this morning………"

"What the fuck shite is this……..", Snapped Davie, as the captain held out a stopping hand towards him.

"Davie please…. let the man finish."

The inspector continued, "Can you gentlemen confirm that you played poker in the Blue Dragon last night and that you also got into a fight with the deceased Mr Ramirez?"

Davie answered, "Sure we played poker there, but I would hardly call it a fight. One of the guys was cheating at cards and, well, I don't know how you people deal with a cheat at cards but where we come from its deserving of a smack in the puss."

The inspector looked quizzically at Davie", "The puss, did you say?"

"Yes…. oh sorry, a Scottish term, it means the face." Explained Davie.

"And as far as you gentlemen are concerned that is all that happened?"

"That is all, that happened." Emphasized Tam, "We then left and went on into your lovely City."

"I'm sorry Gentlemen but I have three witnesses who will testify that when you left the Blue Dragon you proceeded to go around the back where Mr Ramirez had been taken, whereupon Mr Goodison stabbed the victim at least three times to the body."

"Well, there's just one problem I can see with that inspector," protested Davie, "Neither the two of us carries any knives."

The Inspector then turned to the two constables and said something in Spanish, whereupon the two men indicated to Tam to raise his arms to be searched.

Davie laughed, "Yer waistin' yer time I told ye we don't carry kni……"

Davie starred, in astonishment as one of the constables removed the flick knife from Tam's pocket.

"What the fuck Tam? Where the fuck did you get that?" Demanded Davie.

Tam's head was lowered, "Last night the fat dealer guy tried tae stab you and his knife……. that knife, stuck in the top of the table and………and I took it during the stramash."

Davie held up a couple of stopping hands, "Wait a minute, wait a minute, Tam having this knife disnae mean he stabbed anybody…... and by the way, how did you guys know to come after us, to our ship."

Before answering Davie, the Inspector once again said something in Spanish to one of the Constables who then left the room.

"As I said before Mr Harley, we have witnesses. Witnesses who heard you tell Mr Ramirez that you were sailors and that you were Scottish. There is only one ship in the harbour from Scotland the "Empress of the Clyde". The witnesses also heard you use each other's names."

Just then the Constable returned and to Tam and Davies utter amazement he had one of the witnesses with him and both the lads immediately recognised the man..........it was the fat clumsy dealer.

"Gentlemen, this is Manuel Ramirez, Brother of the deceased, do you know this man?" Asked the Inspector.

"Yes, we do Inspector, this is the man who helped the deceased cheat at cards and owned the knife." Said Davie, a slight hint of anger in his voice.

"I see Mr Harley; I also see that this angers you. I'm sure, just as it angered you last night. In fact, it angered the both of you so much that you felt the need for retribution, went out the back of the building and Mr Goodison with his newfound knife took that retribution out on Mr Jose Ramirez."

"That's a fucking lie!" Shouted Tam as he leaned towards the Inspector.

Seeing Tams Rage, the Inspector then removed a pistol from his belt and ordered the two Constables to take Tam and Davie away.

The Spirit of St. Andrew

"Just a minute!" Demanded Captain McNeil, "These men are British subjects and right now technically you Policemen are on British soil……so, I don't think you have the right to take them out of here!"

"Captain McNeil, I admire your loyalty to your men, but let me assure you, if you keep these men here your ship will be stopped from ever leaving this port. I give you my word on that." Was the Inspectors terse reply.

Davie interrupted, "Look Captain we'll go we them. This is a load o' shite anyway, they canny prove what never happened."

Before they knew it Tam and Davie were traveling through the streets of Savanta, heading for the local Police jail. They were still wearing the shirt and trousers from the previous night. As they gazed from the window, Tam was quite taken by the number of red banners bearing the German swastika hanging from many different buildings.

"Here Davie, I dinny remember all they flags the last time we were here, this guy Ramon has gone big time on this Nazi shite."

"Sorry Tam but I've got other things tae occupy my mind just now, like, how the fuck did we end up in this……murder b' Christ!" Replied a rather nervous Davie.

"Och Davie, never mind, Captain McLean will soon sort it oot."

"Oh, dae ye think. Ah think he's got mare on his mind like getting' tae hell oot o' this fuckin' dump."

Their car drew up at a rather dull looking stone building that had POLICE written above the doorway in Spanish. The lads were taken to the front desk and were read the charges against them then taken down some stairs to the cells. Again, it reminded Davie of something out of a western movie. Iron bar cells in a line with a stone wall containing small, barred windows at the top. They were put in together which pleased the lads as they would at least have each other for company, and to discuss all that goes on and what to do about the whole sordid situation quietly between themselves.

They weren't long there when an official looking chap came to see them. He had a rather hard looking middle-aged woman with him whom they both assumed was his secretary as she had pencil and paper in hand. Two seats were set outside their cell and they communicated through the bars.

He was a well-dressed man, fitted out in a standard white suit with shirt and tie. He was balding, about fifty and very lean. The woman wore a grey suit which didn't seem to sit well on her probably due to her "dumpy" shape Davie thought. Davie and Tam sat on the edge of their beds to get as close and as comfortable as possible.

"Gentlemen, you will have to forgive me, my Eenglish is not that good, but I will try my best. My name is Ronaldo Cordoba and my assistant, he glanced at the woman, is

Angela, (who forced a smile from the side of her mouth) I have been appointed by the State to represent you at trial."

"Hold on, hold on," Demanded Davie, as he held up a hand towards Mr Cordoba, "We have done nothing of this. Our ship is due to leave tomorrow, and we are stuck in this dump on the word of some fat bastard who is probably the one that did the killing."

It was the turn of their lawyer to hold up a hand towards Davie, "Signor, you can make these demands until you are…what is it you say……blue in the face. What will be looked at is the evidence and believe me Signor it is all stacked against you. You assaulted the dead man in the Blue Dragon, you were seen leaving just as the man who was killed was taken out, and, most critically you friend here has the murder weapon on his person."

"So, Mr Lawyer, what is the likely outcome to all this?" Asked Tam.

The Lawyer hesitated for a few seconds, "Gentlemen, the law in Beldovia is very clear when it comes to murder, quite simply, it is the death penalty."

"What!" Shouted Tam, "There going to kill us?"

The Lawyer just stared a vacant stare at Davie and Tam.

"Hold on, hold on," Said Davie, "Surely it's just our word against this damned useless dealer, ah mean we can get references from our ship about our character, from the British consulate..."

"Signor..." Interrupted Mr Cordoba, "The state has three witnesses, not just the one."

"What.... wait a minute, you mean there were three Beldovians who stood and watched one of their countrymen getting stabbed to death and they did nothing?" Asked a rather bemused Tam.

"Well Signor, they may say they are doing something now." Was the terse reply.

"Ok, ok," Said Davie, "So, what's the next step?"

"A date will be set for your trial; I would say in about a week. So, I would suggest you get all the references you can together because I must tell you, it does not look good gentlemen."

"A week!" Shouted Davie, "Our bloody boat will be away in a couple of days, if by some miracle we are found not guilty, what the hell do we do then?"

The lawyer stood up and just shrugged his shoulders before leaving.

He was only away about ten minutes when the lads were delighted to see Captain McNeil approach their cell and sit where the lawyer had sat.

"Jesus Captain are we glad to see you." Uttered Tam.

"Well, don't get to excited lads I'm afraid I've only got bad news." he shuffled in his chair, "The thing is I've just come from the British consulate where they informed me that Britain is only a couple of days from breaking of diplomatic relations from Beldovia. There holding off these two days to allow time for all our ships to get to hell out of here, I'm sorry lad's."

"You're sorry, well, let me tell you Captain you're not half as sorry as the poor fuckers sittin' hear facin' a death sentence!" Exclaimed Davie.

"Look," McNeil went on, "The consulate is sending them a letter demanding that you are British subjects and should be delt with in our country. They'll say you'll be treated as harshly back home as you would be here if found guilty. Other than that, I don't know what I can say lads, of course I've left excellent character references with them……. So, who knows."

"Who knows, who knows, I fuckin' know," Shouted Tam, "These bastards will string us up as quick as blink an eye, aye, and do you know what makes it worse, our own fuckin' country only goes and breaks of relations just as were about to go on trial for our fuckin' lives, makin' these bastards hate us all the more, well thanks a lot Britain."

Davie puts his hand on Tam's shoulder, "Look mate, us two the 'gether have come through the bloody Great War, we even near got shipwrecked of the Cape o' good hope, remember, so, this, this is chickenfeed for us, mere chickenfeed."

CHAPTER 11.
TRIAL.

Ten days passed, the "Empress of The Clyde" had left a week previous, a day before diplomatic relations were indeed severed between Britain and Beldovia.

Davie and Tam were brought up from the cells and stood in the dock. Davie looked around and thought the court much like any he had seen back home.

The judge entered and everyone stood up. Tam took a good hard look at the man. He was quite small and plump, and the late August heat seemed to be making him sweat as he wiped his forehead with a hankie.

The lads pleaded not guilty, although they had a very strong foreboding about the whole thing. They were even more shocked when another witness, other than the fat dealer, turned out to be one of the peasants who was losing money to the man in the suit at the card table.

Davie leaned over to Tam, "What a cowardly fuckin' weasel, ah actually gave that bastard money that night."

Davie had had enough as he stood up and shouted at the peasant, "Ye backstabbing bastard, what did ye spend the money ah gave ye on, fuckin' white feathers ye bastard. Oh aye……….and where's yer we pal, sharpenin' e's knife for yer next victim ye murderin' we bastard!"

"Silesia, silensia! Shouted the Judge as he banged his gavel on his desk.

"Agh silence yersel', ye fat sweaty bastard, this is no a court o' justice it's a fuckin' kangaroo court."

The lads lawyer then turned to speak to them, "Gentlemen you only make things worse…....please."

"Make things worse, how much fuckin' worse could it get… what? are they going to hang us twice or something." Said Davie.

Worse was indeed to come as a statement from the other peasant was read out, saying that Tam and Davie are the guilty party. Mr Cordoba turned and explained to the lads the second peasant had asked the court's leave as his ship was leaving harbour.

"My God, "Said Tam, "The wee bastard's a fellow mariner and he still knifes us in the back".

Sure enough, a guilty verdict was returned and sure enough the judge adorned his head with the black cap as he passed sentence.

As he spoke in Spanish their Lawyer translated.

The Spirit of St. Andrew

"You men committed a heinous crime when you struck down a defenceless man, I therefor have no option but to sentence you to death by hanging at the Phillipe Ramon Penitentiary within a period of two weeks. This will allow any time for an appeal before sentence is carried out. And may the Lord have mercy on your soul."

Davie and Tam were taken back to their cell where they asked their Lawyer why the sentence wasn't being carried out where they were.

"There are no facilities for such an up-taking here Gentlemen that is why you are being sent to the Phillipe Ramon Penitentiary where they have gallows at the ready."

"And where the hell is this, penitentiary?" Demanded Tam.

"Oh, it is a very special place that is stuck in the middle of the rainforest, "The Hellhole" your soon to be fellow inmates call it, and when you get there, you will see why gentlemen."

"Ok Mr Cordoba looks like we're pretty well fucked. Before we go though, I'd like to send a letter back home to my son and daughter." Said Davie, to which the Lawyer agreed.

"I will get you pen and paper, but now that I think about it, how will your letter get back to Britain?"

"I thought of that," Said Davie, "I noticed other ships in the harbour, one from France, one from Holland. I'm sure they would move the letter on when they returned home."

"Ok, signor, I'll get that done for you." Said Cordoba, as he made to leave.

Davie and Tam were then left on their own, "Well Mr Harley, this looks like the end of the line for us lads."

Davie immediately sprang to his feet and went right into Tam's face, "Don't you ever dare talk like that. We are going to get oot of this no matter what it takes, do you hear Mr Goodison."

"Oh aye, and just what the fuck are we going tae dae, dig a tunnel ah the way back tae Bonnie Dundee, or what?"

"Dinny be fuckin' stupid Tam, we only need to dig it to Brazil. Yer a hell of a bugger tae exaggerate." Quipped Davie.

"No, but seriously Tam, we are going to look at every opportunity that comes our way between now and….and…well whenever, tae get oorsel's oot oh this fuckin' mess."

A couple of days later Davie and Tam were lying across their bunks when Mr Cordoba and his female assistant approached their cell.

"Well, well, if it isn't Sherlock Holmes and Betty Grable come to tell us they've got us off Scot free". Said Tam sarcastically.

"Tam! Nay need," Cautioned Davie, "Ignore my pal Mr Cordoba he's no had his porridge yet."

Cordoba just gave the briefest of smiles before he sat down and opened out some papers, he had with him.

"You gentlemen will be taken from here in two days' time to the Phillipe Ramon Penitentiary, there to await execution."

"Ok Mr Cordoba, I know I asked you before, but just where and what is this Penitentiary?" Asked Davie.

"Right gentlemen, if you sit down, I will tell you."

Davie and Tam sat on the ends of their bunks and gave the Lawyer their full attention.

"There's a man in Beldovia, his name doesn't matter, who is a great pilot, he styles himself after the great Charles Lindbergh. He would take Mr Ramon our president on long flights just to impress him. On one such flight over the rainforest they spotted a clearing which it would seem, had been opened by native Indians and abandoned. A river run alongside the opening and the pilot said to Mr Ramon, "Sir, that would be a great place to dump some of your convicts. Surprisingly Mr Ramon took the pilots word to heart and set about building a prison."

The Spirit of St. Andrew

"How the hell did they manage that, out in the middle of nowhere?" Quizzed Tam.

"Ah, you may well ask. Firstly he had to get permission from Brazil, after all it is in their territory, so Signor Ramon obtained a 100-year lease. Next, how do you get people on the ground, not to mention tools etc;. It was done very cleverly, firstly five well-armed men were parachuted in to clear a landing place for the planes. Fortunately, the natives had opened up a large area, all that remained was for these men to make sure it was level and smooth enough for a landing. It took them five days. Well, now that planes could land it was easier to bring in men, tools, and supplies."

"So, the whole place is built with wood from the rainforest, but, surly that would take a lot of time to chop down trees……ah mean, how did they mill the timber?" Asked Davie.

"As you know gentlemen by this time Phillipe Ramon was friendly with Adolf Hitler and he had a company in Germany named Stihl, you may have heard of them?"

Davie and Tam looked at each other before Davie suddenly thought, "Ah yes, chainsaws, they make these new chainsaw things."

"What the fuck is a chainsaw?" Asked a puzzled looking Tam.

"Oh Tam, their brilliant, they cut the fuck through a tree in seconds."

The Spirit of St. Andrew

"Wow!" Said Tam, looking a little bedazzled.

"As well as chainsaws they brought in a generator. It was large and the plane had to be emptied of everything so it could handle the weight. Before long convicts were being flown in to do the work and within four years it was more or less complete. In fact, now, they are building an extended part for some new special prisoners at the bequest of Adolf Hitler."

"Special prisoners?" Quizzed Davie.

"Yes, though you'll probably find out who, when you arrive there gentlemen." Said Cordoba as he rose to go.

"Hold on," shouted Tam, "You haven't said anything about our appeal, or on what day we will actually be murdered."

Cordoba stopped, "Oh sorry gentlemen, I forgot, your appeal

was rejected."

"What! Hey, get back here!" Tam shouted, but to no avail, Cordoba just kept walking.

Tam sat back down, "What did he say, stuck in the middle of the rainforest."

"So, at least there'll be plenty o' places tae take a shite Tam." Jibed Davie, to which Tam whacked him with his pillow.

CHAPTER 12.
THE HELLHOLE.

Davie and Tam had never flow before and it had to be said they were quite enjoying the experience. They were on board a Stinson Tri-Motor plane, capable of carrying a pilot and 10 passengers, as well as other baggage. It was a lovely clear day and as well as Davie and Tam, there were four other new prisoners heading for the Penitentiary as well as four guards. They would be relieving four others when the plane returned, along with prisoners whose time had been served.

As they looked over the vastness of the rainforest, one of the guards who spoke English said, "Surely you have never seen anything so vast in all your life Signor?"

"Yes, I have." Said Davie.

The guard smirked, "Oh yes, and what would that be, surely there is nothing greater!"

"Well, I've seen a couple of oceans, for starters."

The Spirit of St. Andrew

Tam smiled at Davies answer as he looked out of the window next to Davie, "Mind you Davie, that is some size of a forest. If we did somehow get away from this "Hellhole", how the fuck do we get out of that monstrosity there's miles and miles of it. The only other thing I can see other than tree's is a couple of rivers running through it.?"

"Yer right Tam, the thing is though, if we are in that forest, it would mean we are still alive."

"That's true mate, and where there's life, there's hope."

As the plane started to descend the "Hellhole" came into view.

The dimensions reminded Davie of an oversized football pitch with five large rectangular shaped wooden huts adjacent to each other running down each side. At the opposite end, away from the river, which past it, were two other large huts which Davie assumed would be where the men ate, and the guards were billeted. Also, just as Cordoba had told them there were new huts being built just outside the perimeter fence.

Tam and Davie had to agree it was quite a feat of engineering.

It was a bumpy landing, before the plane taxied up to the gates of the prison. Two large wooden gates to be exact, both about six feet wide and ten feet high with chain-link wire over them, both lying open, for their arrival Davie presumed. Guards ascended on the light aircraft and

The Spirit of St. Andrew

escorted the prisoners into the compound where they were told to wait in a line. Another guard appeared carrying what looked like a pile of clothing. Sure enough, a suit of black and white striped shirt and trousers that were laid at the feet of each new prisoner. The guards were all dressed in dark blue short sleeved uniforms and carried batons in their hands and had pistols strapped to their waists. Davie and Tam watched as other inmates made their way towards them, obviously curious to see who had arrived. They were all dressed in vertically striped black and white outfits just like the ones laid out for them.

Other guards told the men to keep back before all eyes turned towards one of the large sheds. The door had opened and a rather large overweight man in a brown uniform alighted.

It didn't take a genius to figure out that this was the camp governor. He was a man who looked in his fifties, wearing the standard black moustache which most men in this country seemed to sport. To Davie and Tam, the man looked tired, almost uninterested. He waved a hand towards the guards as if to say, "Keep those men back", as he approached the new inmates which of course included our two Scotsmen.

First in Spanish, then in English he introduced himself as Captain Sanchez, then ordered the men to strip naked and put on the uniform that had been laid out in front of them, which all the men did.

For the benefit of the other new inmates, he started off speaking in Spanish before slipping in to English, saying that he would attend to Davie and Tam in a moment. As he spoke Davie and Tam watched as the guards removed all their clothes from the ground and took then to the other large hut at the end of the compound.

Sure enough, it was only a few minutes before he turned towards the lads. As he did the Spanish speakers all left to go to their appropriate huts.

"Gentlemen, you are here because you committed a heinous crime against one of the citizens of Beldovia and for this you will pay the ultimate prise."

"No, we did not, we were stich………." Tam didn't get to finish as he was whacked across the back with a baton by one of the guards.

"Ye bastard!" Winced Tam, as he turned to hit out, only to see that two guard were ready to deliver again.

"You men will not speak unless I invite you too." Said the Governor, before continuing, "You will be placed in the hut with all the other foreign nationals, there to await your execution, the exact date of which I do not yet have. Rest assured though it will not be a long period of time, two to three days at most. Until then you will receive two meals a day. Oatmeal in the morning and a cooked meal at night. As you can see gentlemen there is a fence of wire around the encampment. You may think you can make your way through this fence. The thing is, this fence is not there to keep you in, although it helps, no, the fence is there to keep the wild natives and animals out. You must realise gentlemen that escape is futile, for beyond the bounds of this encampment there is a thousand deaths awaiting you, if not at the hands of the cannibalistic natives, then certainly from the numerous wild animals that are within the rainforest." He went on, "Furthermore, if you gentlemen care to look to the top of the compound you will see that the top end sits open. This is because there is no need for fencing as there is a ravine at that end where the river flows. It has about a 50-foot drop, straight down to jagged rocks below, so really, there is no need for fencing. None-the-less it is forbidden to go near the edge. You will see that there is a small "trip" fence about ten feet back from the edge, no prisoner is allowed over that fence which is always patrolled by guards.

He continued, "There are other rules that you must adhere to in the short time you will be here. No violence will be tolerated within the compound or the huts. Depending on the severity of any violence, will depend on the punishment. If you look to your left gentlemen, you will see a small tin hut. It is extremely hot and uncomfortable inside, and this is the solitary confinement hut which is where a man is placed if he is in anyway violent, the length of time spent there will depend on my good grace. Extreme violence resulting in a man's death, will result in the guilty party being executed, if fact we have one such punishment being handed out tomorrow gentlemen so you will have a ring side seat to this. Further

The Spirit of St. Andrew

on from the tin hut as you can see work is being carried out on the hangman's scaffold, which is where you two men will most likely meet your maker. Now, the guards will show you to your hut, that is all!"

As they walked towards their hut Davie was taken by the strange reception they were being given by the other prisoners. Some were trying to pat Davie and Tam on the back, while other were spitting at their feet.

"Welcome to hut four, gentlemen." Said a tall thin man in a very Englified voice, the man then holding out a hand to shake, "My name is William Smythe, that's Smythe with a "Y"."

Tam shook his hand, "Tam Goodison, that's Goodison with an "oo"."

Smythe just grinned at Tam's comment before turning to Davie who also shook his hand," Davie Harley, with a….a….nothing really."

The lads gazed inside the long hut which had five sets of double bunk beds down either side, thus catering for twenty men. At the far end they could see a long metal trough which had a couple of taps feeding it, this no doubt for washing. At the side was a small cubical which they figured housed a toilet. At the end they stood at, was an iron stove fuelled by wood. There were a couple of pots on top of the stove giving the men hot water when required.

Davie went on, "So, what are you in for Mr Smythe?"

"Please, call me Bill……. I'm a political prisoner. Outside I'm a journalist, I wrote a rather scathing article about Phillipe Ramon, to which he took exception and threw me in here for six months. Times up in a couple of days actually, if these buggers stick to the rules."

"And all these other blokes in here….?" Asked Tam, as he looked around at the many faces staring out towards the new inmates.

"Some are like me; others are in for repeated petty crimes. Of the 200 prisoners in the "Hellhole", most are the worst of Beldovia's criminal factions, although we do have a revolutionary named Carlos Vegas who was sent here for stirring up the people of Beldovia to rebel against Ramon, I believe he still has quite a following in Savanta. Anyway, that is what this place was constructed for, the worst of the worst. Too often in the small prison back in Savanta there were escapes by criminals back into the city. Even the drug dealers and gangsters were finding it too easy to continue running their schemes from the prison. Something needed to be done, and so we have the "Hellhole" or The Phillipe Ramon Penitentiary".

"I noticed we got quite a varied reception from the inmates as we made our way here, what was all that about Bill?" Asked Davie.

"Ah, well," Said Smythe, "You see the man you killed…."

Tam was quick to cut in, "We didn't, kill him."

The Spirit of St. Andrew

Bill held up an apologetic hand, "Sorry, the man that was killed was a drug dealer stroke money lender of not very great repute, so there were those who were glad to see the back of him, while other's in here are friends who worked for him. That is why I would say, watch your backs while you are here."

"The Governor said something about us having a ring side seat to an execution tomorrow. Is there going to be a hanging?" Asked Tam.

"No no, there will be an execution by firing squad. Some poor bastard will be taken to the top of the compound where he will be shot in the back and thrown over the ravine to the rocks below, there, his body will be taken care of by the wildlife of the forest." Said Smythe.

That evening, Davie and Tam lay on their bunk beds talking quietly to each other.

"Here Tam……." said Davie, "…..You know, we could, if these bastards get their way, be dead in a few days or so. Have you nae regrets that ye never married had a couple o' bairns. Ah mean you're a no bad lookin' man of near six foot in stature and yer still just in yer late thirties………. ah ken yer no a poof or that, ah mean yer never away fae the brothels in all the ports".

Tam was quiet for a few seconds, "Well, Mr Harley, it may surprise you tae know that I very nearly got married once."

"Seriously?" Quizzed Davie.

"Aye seriously. Durin' the War, ah was eighteen, near nineteen, I was at the Empress Ballroom near the docks in Dundee when I saw the most gorgeous creature that ever walked the earth. Her name was Kathleen McGuire, she was Irish, and her parents had come over for work in the Dundee jute mills. I thought a beauty like that'll never give me the time o' day but ah still plucked up the courage tae go and ask her tae dance. Well, ye could o' knocked me ower we a feather when she said aye."

"What happened?"

"What happened," Repeated Tam, "The bloody war, that's what happened, or at least my involvement in it. We baith fell head ower heels for each other until I got my "call up" papers through. Kathleen wanted tae marry afore ah left but ah said no, ah mean, ah didnae ken what the hell was goin' tae happen and ah didnae want Kathleen bein' a widow afore we'd barely got married. It near broke our hearts sayin' goodbye at the station and that was the last ah saw o' her."

"Jesus, what happened Tam?"

"As you know Davie, I got badly wounded in France. So badly wounded that some daft bastard threw my body in we the dead jist like you. Fortunately, ah managed tae raise a hand and somebody saw I was still alive. The thing was though my papers had been passed on to those who notify the next of kin. When my mother got the telegram saying I had been "Killed in action" she of course told

Kathleen, who was devastated. They told me she was quite inconsolable."

"So, what happened Tam?" Said a now engrossed Davie.

Tam hesitated for quite a while, "She walked out on to the Tay rail bridge and threw herself off."

"Jesus!"

"You know Davie, my mother received the telegram saying that I was still alive the same day Kathleen went off the bridge."

"Jesus Tam, I'm really sorry aboot that, you never telt me before." Said Davie.

"Aye well, ah swore ah would never get as close as that to a woman again. Ah couldnae go through that again, damned well broke my heart. Still ye never know ah may well meet up we Kathleen in a couple o' days, who knows!"

"Aye Tam, ye never know."

Davie thought for a moment about Tam's strange tale before getting back to their present dilemma, "Listen Tam, over the next two days we are going to have to look at every situation in this place to find ways of getting' tae hell oot o' here."

"Aye right Davie, but to hell oot tae where...... the bloody jungle we ah they murderin' natives and beast o' ah kinds.

It's a bit o' the Devil or the deep blue see, if ye ask me mate!" Replied Tam.

"Maybe yer right Mate, but for as long as we can, we'll still be alive and fighting'."

The next morning it was pouring rain and the camp was roused early. It had been decided the execution would take place before breakfast as they didn't want men peucking all over the compound after the sight they were about to see.

The guards formed a central gap running up between the men as the poor condemned man was brought out between two guards who were holding an arm each. The man looked desolate and terrified as he wriggled between the two guards. His voice was pleading to be forgiven which of course was falling on deaf ears. Behind the man were another two guards carrying rifles.

Davie and Tam were right at the top of the compound as near to the "trip" fence as they dared get. Davie was up there with an ulterior motive as he backed himself into the mass of men who were there. Davie had decided he wanted to see what lay beyond the top of the ravine and he knew he had to get a lot closer than the "trip" fence to do so. He watched as the two-armed guards patrolling that area watching all the men milling around.

Suddenly there was a slight surge as the prisoner drew nearer to the top and the guards stare turned away towards that.

The Spirit of St. Andrew

"Nows my chance", thought Davie, and, quick as a flash, he jumped over the trip fence and before he knew it, he was gazing into the ravine. First to catch his eye was the large waterfall fall just beyond the perimeter fence to his left. It dropped into a huge pool of black water almost directly beneath him. The darkness told Davie that this had to be quite deep. The pool threw out its water downstream to what were rocks and boulders which was probably where the condemned man was about to be dropped.

"Hoi!" Shouted the guard at Davie as he scurried towards him. Davie immediately threw his hands in the air and made to cross back over the "trip" fence. When the guard arrived, he thumped Davie in the back with the butt of his gun and shouted something in Spanish towards him to the effect that you do not go over the fence.

Davie returned to the relative safety of the crowd just as the rain started to subside. The poor victim was now stood having his hand cuffs removed before all his clothes were taken from him. He was mumbling some sort of prayer as he cried uncontrollably. The execution was almost genius in its simplicity. The two guards still had him by an arm each as they approached the edge of the ravine.

Captain Sanchez shouted out some words in Spanish which Davie and Tam took to mean sentence was about to be carried out. Sanchez stepped back as the two riflemen took aim at the accused who stood blubbering as urine ran down his leg. Despite knowing what was coming most of the men still jumped when the rifles went off. A vapour cloud of blood and bodily tissue burst out from the victim's chest causing a groaning sound from the onlookers. The accused then slumped downwards, before the two guards dropped his body over the ravine.

There was a silent pause for a moment before Captain Sanchez order the men be dispersed for breakfast.

"Jesus Davie, that was a bit barbaric don't you think. I mean, I've seen things in the War, but that, that was up there with them." Said Tam.

"Aye Tam, just the thing tae give ye good appetite for breakfast." Replied Davie.

"Anyway Davie," Continued Tam, "what did you find out up there?"

"Later Tam, later."

After breakfast the lads were back at their hut when two guards approached.

"Oh oh……..", Said Tam, in a suspicious manner, "…….incoming."

The guards came right up to Davie and Tam and indicated to them to follow. They were marched straight to Captain Sanchez office. The two lads stood in front of his desk as he read some letter before looking up.

The Spirit of St. Andrew

"Gentlemen, I have received word that your execution will take place in three days' time, whereupon you will be hanged at the gallows."

He then paused briefly before telling Tam he was excused. One of the guards took Tam by the arm to escort him out, as he did Tam stared at Dave who looked back with as much bemusement as Tam who was now shrugging his shoulders.

Sanchez eventually looked up at Davie, "Mr Harley, you are to spend 36 hours in the solitary confinement shed, reason being that you were seen to cross the "trip" fence at the top of the compound which is in violation of the rules."

"What?" Shouted Davie, "Are you serious, you're going to murder me in three days. What the fuck difference will it make to me being cooped up for 36 hours?"

"We have rules here Mr Harley, if the prisoners see you getting away with this violation what kind of a signal would that be sending out to the rest of the men?" Retorted Sanchez.

He then ordered the guards to take Davie away. He was taken to the tin hut Sanchez showed them on their arrival. Davie wasn't liking this one little bit, apart from the heat he felt building for the day, Davie was very claustrophobic and was not looking forward to this at all.

The first thing to hit him when they shut him in was the thickness of the air and the heat making it hard to breath comfortably. It was pitch dark except for a couple of minute streaks of light coming through two nail holes in the corrugated iron. Davie was struggling to keep himself calm as he crawled to the corner where the tiny beads of light were shing through. He battled to calm himself by thinking of home, his family, happy times, anything to get control.

Eventually he settled and got to grips with his breathing by taking in slow deep breaths and letting them out slowly. He had to fight off the impending desire to want to kick out the corrugated sheeting which he felt he could easily dislodge, but he knew they would just repair it and probably increase his duration in the confined area.

Davie thought long about his beloved Jean and the great times they had on the farm. Wonderful days they spent in Aberdeen at the beach and at Duthie park. These thoughts were proving to be lifesavers for a man trapped in a small, extremely hot prison cell.

Now that Davie had control of his mind, he started to think of how in the hell he and Tam were going to get away from this place and even if they did, just how were they going to survive the rainforest and even harder, how were they going to get back to any kind of civilisation when they were a minimum of 50 to 75 miles in any direction from such things.

The time passed and eventually Davie heard the guards at the door of his small prison. The light was the first thing to hit Davie as he crawled from the isolation unit. He cupped a hand over his eyes and blinked fervently until his eyes adapted.

As he stood up the first person to greet him was his friend Tam.

"Well Mr Harley, how lucky are you, being released just in time for your own hanging."

"Cheers Tam, you certainly know how to build a blokes spirit." Replied Davie, who then realised there was a gathering of the men at the foot of the compound across from the guard's quarters.

"What the hell's going on?" He asked, just as William Smythe approached.

"Davie, the prisoners are getting quite well entertained by the hangman trying to finish the repairs of his gallows." Said Tam, a slight grin to his face.

Davie looked across and saw this small black-haired man dishing out orders to guards. The gallows were raised about ten feet from ground level and Davie could see that the trapdoor from where they wound drop was open.

Davie was studying the hangman when a realisation came over him.

"Jesus Tam, take a good look at that bugger......now, who the hell does he remind you of?"

Tam stared at the hangman for a few seconds.... Jesus Davie, it's Charlie bloody Chaplin!"

The Spirit of St. Andrew

A broad smile came across Davies face, "My thought exactly Tam."

The next surprise came when Davie and Tam could see the hangman pointing in their direction which was followed by two guards approaching them and directing them towards the hangman.

The hangman only came up to about Davie and Tams shoulders as he gazed up at them and spoke in very bad English.

Looking firstly at Davie he asked, " What iz your height signor?"

"Six feet." Replied Davie.

"No no, centimetre, centimetre!"

Davie looked puzzled for he knew no more about centimetre than the Hangman knew about feet and inches, "Sent-to-meet who?" Puzzled Davie.

This caused a laugh to break out among the men gathered around the scaffold.

"No no," The Hangman shouted before he held his hand up to Davie's height and seemed to take a guess before writing on his piece of paper.

He then turned to Tam, "Your weight Signor?"

"Fourteen stones seven pounds." Relied Tam.

"No no no!" Replied the Hangman a frustration in his voice, "Kilogram, kilogram!"

Tam looked as puzzled as Davie had about his height.

"Sure, I'd love to send a telegram." Replied Tam.

The poor Hangman was now bereft as the crowd of men all laughed once more.

He just wrote something on his paper before heading back to the gallows where he climbed the steps to the platform. All the men were watching him as he stood shaking his head in dismay at what had just taken place. As he wrote he kept walking and was unaware of a length of rope he had been preparing was left lying on the platform. To everyone's entertainment he tripped on the rope and fell forward through the open trapdoor hitting his head on the far side on the way down. Such was the crack made when his head hit the far side that the crowd of men gasped with anguish. When he reached the ground, he never moved as blood started to flow from a rather nasty cut right across his forehead. The guards all ran to his aid, but it didn't take a genius to figure out that this chap would not be conducting any hanging ceremony any time soon.

Davie and Tam looked on and laughed along, as Tam said, "Jesus Davie, this guy's funnier that Chaplin, he's in the wrong business."

CHAPTER 13.
EXECUTION.

Not long after the escapade with the Hangman, Davie and Tam were once more summoned to the captain's office. It came as no surprise when they were told that they were not to be hanged after all as the Hangman had met with a rather nasty accident.

"So, Gentlemen, it has been decided that you will now be shot in the same method as you saw carried out the other day at the top of the ravine."

"And when will this take place?" Asked Davie.

"First thing tomorrow morning, that is all." Said Sanchez as he waved a hand to the guards to take Davie and Tam away.

"Hang on," Said Davie, "Were British citizens, what's to happen to our bodies after you murder us. We want them sent back home to our families."

Sanchez cut in, "You Gentlemen gave up all those rites when you killed a citizen of this country. As it is, your

The Spirit of St. Andrew

Country will be notified of your execution. Take them away."

That night in their hut, Davie and Tam were in full confab with William Smythe and another couple of the men they felt they could rely on. A plan was being hatched, a plan that was nothing short of desperate, but as Davie said to them, "These are desperate times."

The other prisoners were surprised to see Davie and Tam eat a hearty breakfast. The porridge was never very special, but the lads were stuffing as Mutch of it away as they could.

The guards came for them as the camp was assembled for an execution. Hut number four was at the bottom end, so they had to be marched at least 50 yards to where their cuffs would be removed. As they walked Davie and Tam felt the firm hands of the guards at each side of them. They also noted the two riflemen behind them and nodded to each other in a way that said, ye, everything is fine up to now.

There was an eerie quiet among the prisoners as they made their way ever closer to the point of execution. Davie could see those who sneered towards them as well as those who looked on compassionately.

Soon they stopped at the point where they knew they would be uncuffed and there clothing removed. Sure enough, they were unfettered, and as their tops were taken off a scuffle broke out amongst the men. Four men rolled out from the line on top of other men who were cursing wildly as they all fell to the open ground between all the others. The guards, both beside Davie and Tam, and at the top of the ravine turned their attention towards the incident which looked as if it was becoming violent. It was being instigated by those who were within Davie and Tams hut, just as they had requested them to do.

Without hesitation, Davie and Tam, on seeing that the guards attending to them, were also distracted, quickly and firmly tugged their right arm loose and swung a couple of right hooks square on the jaw of two of the men and immediately pushed the other two into the two guards who were to have shot the lads. Now free of the shackles and the guards, in an instant, they sprinted towards the ravine. A gap was open where the guards had pushed men back and Davie and Tam were on to it in a flash. Some prisoners seeing what was happening made to help Davie and Tam by blocking the paths of the guards who were in total disarray. Captain Sanchez was screaming at the top of his voice for them to be stopped.

All hell was breaking loose as guards turned in different directions to see what the hell was going on. As it was, Davie and Tam were now at the top of the ravine and without a second's hesitation leapt right over the edge.

For Tam, it was a complete leap of faith. Faith in his friend, that where they were jumping to was freedom, nothing more, nothing less.

Tam's breath was dragged form his body as he watched the black pool of water rise to meet him at great speed. As Davie fell, he prayed to the Almighty that it was indeed deep water that they were headed for and not a mass of gagged rocks only a couple of feet beneath the surface.

To Davies relief the two plunged deep into the water, the instant cold causing them to fight to hold their breath. As they touched bottom with their feet, Davie tugged at Tams arm and pointed, to let Tam know they had to swim as far as possible under water to the far side. Tam nodded and the two set off. What awaited them when they broke surface was indeed a surprise. They fully expected to be shot at by the guards and that they would be on a wing and a prayer as to whether they would be hit.

To their utter surprise, not one shot wrang out, instead all they heard was Captain Sanchez shouting out at them.

"Don't worry, I will not waist one bullet on you, not one. I leave you to die a thousand deaths at the hand of the rainforest."

"That's quite gracious of him Davie....don't you think?" Quipped Tam, as the two of them crawled up through a dark muddy embankment to the far side of the riverbank and into the rainforest.

"Always thought he was good guy, Tam."

Once they were safely into the shelter of the trees Davie and Tam danced around in a circle like some form of highland fling whooping and shouting for all their worth both covered in the dark gooey mud.

"We fuckin' did it Davie, we fuckin' only fuckin' did it!" Roared Tam with utter delight.

As he did the two fell to the ground to gather themselves, breathing heavily they both lay back with huge grins across their faces, instantly reliving what had just happened.

"Tam, we owe one huge thankyou to the lads that were in our hut for putting on that show. I couldn't see the guards dropping their guard for any other reason. Hope they don't get into too much shit for it."

"Good guys Davie, good guys and I'm glad good old Smythe with a "Y" kept out of it like we said. Don't want his release to be pushed back."

As Tam stopped speaking, he looked across at his friend with nothing on but a pair of trouser and his boots on his feet, then realised he was in the same state of dress and covered in mud, then thought out loud.

"What the fuck now my man?" He asked of Davie.

Davie looked all around and saw nothing but dense forest.

"Looks like we try to make our way through that!" He said, pointing to the dense undergrowth, "surly to Christ we'll come on something or somebody eventually."

"Aye..." Said Tam, "......but let's go down stream a bit and wash this muck aff."

After they did, the two set off on what they thought was an easterly direction. They decided not to run, rather to set a hefty walking pace and see what happens.

They were finding it tough going as the undergrowth was quite thick with branch after branch seeming to want to whack them or tear at them as they went.

"Shoosh!" Said Davie as he stopped suddenly, grabbing Tam's arm as he did.

"What?" Went Tam.

"Didn't you hear that......there's something following us." Continued Davie, lowering his voice as he spoke.

Suddenly some creature gave out quite a roar from what seemed like around 50 feet away.

"Fuck that......." Said Tam as he started to run, "......I'm oot o' here!"

"Aye, me anaw!" And Davie was off as well.

Now the branches were truly whipping into their faces and bodies as they ran recklessly through the undergrowth. They had no idea what direction they were running in and no idea what lay ahead. Both were breathing heavily as Tam, out in front, suddenly fell to the ground with Davie unable to stop himself, fell on top of his companion. They collapsed together in a small clearing, cursing as they fell.

They both crawled over to a huge Mahogany tree and rested up against it, both men breathing heavily.

"What time of day would you say it was Davie?"

"God knows but we've been on the move quite a few hours, must be some time in the afternoon ah guess."

Tam looked around, "Haven't heard that beast again."

"No thank God," Replied Davie, who went on, "I think we should walk on for a bit, nice and quiet like, then find some place to rest up for the night. What do you think Tam?"

"Sounds like a good plan Davie, let's go."

Light was fading when the lads found a small clearing with a lot of leaves and other foliage on the ground which they thought might give them good cover for the night. As Davie pulled leaves around him, he noticed something on the ground that he thought he recognised.

"Here Tam, isn't that Brazil nuts in that big shell?"

"By God Davie ah think Yer right. Didn't we take a load o' them back the last time we were in South America?"

Davie found a couple of rocks and the lads were soon cracking open the shells and feeding themselves on the contents.

The Spirit of St. Andrew

"Here," Said Tam, "Do you think Sanches'll send oot a search party for us tomorrow, Davie?"

"I doubt that very much Tam. Didn't you hear what he shouted from the top o' the ravine........ "Leave us to die a thousand deaths," he shouted.

"That's true mate. Here Davie, I know it's good to be alive, but this fuckin' place gee's me the creeps."

"Aye, me too, but let's see if we can sleep or at least rest up."

The two men curled up under leaves and branches and tried to get rest as the darkness of night closed in. The noise from the rainforest was eerily loud and disheartening. Every crack of a branch or squeal of an animal caused the lads to become alarmed as trying to find sleep seemed nye well impossible.

Both men relived the day's events a thousand time as they drifted in and out of sleep. Furthermore, neither of them had the foggiest idea what was to become of them the next day.

CHAPTER 14.
CAPTIVES.

Davie was in a trench hole curled into a ball, his hands covering his ears to try and stem the thunderous noise of exploding shells which were going off all around him. He seemed to hear someone shout to him above the cacophony of noise and decided to look up. He was horrified to see his old friend Ginger Copperwaith standing with a black hole in his head where his right eye wound have been and another gaping hole at the back of his head.

Suddenly Davie's drill sergeant, McHarg, pushed Ginger aside and started shouting at the top of his voice towards Davie.

"Get up! Get up! You cowardly bastard Harley, get up!"

Davie was shouting back at him, "There dead, there all dead sergeant!"

"Get up Davie…….. hoi, Davie wake up, your back in the trenches mate, wake up."

The Spirit of St. Andrew

Tam, shaking Davie by the arm, caused him to wake with a start.

"Jesus," said Davie, as he started to come to himself, "I was back there alright, poor Ginger shot though the eye just like we saw him, only he was alive........fuckin' weird Tam, really weird."

"Aye well, welcome back to the real-world mate........take a look at yersel' Davie." Said Tam as he nodded toward Davie's body.

Suddenly Davie sprang to his feet, "Ye bastard.... ants, fuckin' thousands o' them!" He shouted as he brushed them off his body as quickly as he could.

"Yip, I was the same........" said Tam, "......and the wee bastards were nipping as well."

"Fuck me so they are!" Came back Davie, as he started to dance around slapping his body, causing Tam to start laughing.

Davie was about to berate Tam when he suddenly stopped, "What the fuck was that?"

"What?" Replied Tam, still with a smile on his face.

"Didn't you hear it........a gun shot in the distance." Said Davie pointing in the direction from where they came.

"Jesus......" Said Tam, "......some poor bastard being shot at the "Hellhole."

The Spirit of St. Andrew

"That's carried a fair distance Mate, I thought we were well away from there."

"Probably been running in circles. If we had any brains Davie, we'd have followed the bloody river. Tell you what Davie, I could go a plate o' that lumpy porridge they serve up right now.........bloody starvin'."

"Aye, me too, and good cool drink o' water as well.........hold on! What is that rustlin' noise comin' towards us Tam?"

"Fuck sake Davie, sounds awffy like some heavy beast making its way here in a hell o' a hurry."

"Were out o' here Tam, let's go!"

No sooner were the words out of Davie's mouth when the lads were of, running through the brush at top speed. All kinds of branches, leaves and twigs of the undergrowth were whipping off them as they went. They went straight, Criss crossed, turned diagonally, just about every direction you could think of and still Tam shouted, "I can still hear whatever the fuck it is Davie, and it's clossin' in!"

Suddenly the undergrowth got a little clearer and the lads seemed to be on a path of some sort. It made running easier but whatever was behind them was getting ever closer.

In an instant, all changed! Davie, who was out in front immediately dropped out of Tam's vision. Before he knew

The Spirit of St. Andrew

it, Tam was dropping to, and right on top of his friend. They had fallen into a pit of some sort. They could see they were around five feet down and wanted out, but the walls of the pit were greasy as they found themselves slithering around in the hole.

The sound that had been following them was suddenly upon them as a large Taper fell into the pit beside them.

"What the fuck is that!" Shouted Tam, as they stood at one side of the pit and watched the animal try to scamper to its feet at the other.

"Don' know......." Said Davie, ".......looks like some kind o' a fuckin' pig."

"Aye," Said Tam, "one fuckin' angry bastard o' a pig!"

The Taper now had the two men in its vision and did not like what it saw as it crouched down into what the lads' thought was an attack posture.

"Am out o' here!" Shouted Tam, who again tried to climb the slippery sides only to slither back down.

The lads then received the shock of their lives, just as it seemed the Taper was about to lounge at them, two long sharp spears penetrated the animals rib cage, causing it to give out the most God-awful death squeal.

Davie and Tam felt a slight relief as their eyes looked up to see the sides of the pit surrounded by native Indians. They both raised their hands as a submissive gesture for fear they might be the next ones speared by whom they now considered their captors.

Davie and Tam remained silent as they heard the natives mumble to each other in the strangest of dialect. Some seemed relaxed, while others looked a bit more aggressive, Davie thought.

After about a minute the blunt end of two spears were offered down to the lads who look hold of them and were pulled from the pit.

The first thing to strike the pair was how much taller they were than the natives. There were about ten of them, none of them over five foot six. They had black hair cropped on a circle around their heads and had what looked like either sticks or bones through their cheek's noses and ears. They were naked but for a form of loin cloth around their private parts. Some of them had bracelets on their upper arms and lower legs as well as beads around their necks. They were all armed with spears bows and arrows and blow pipes of some sort.

They prodded the lads indicating to them to walk on. Four of them led off carrying the Taper upside down with its legs tied to a long branch, the rest were behind Davie and Tam, they held spears at their backs which they prodded into them without breaking the skin but enough to let them know they must keep going.

It did cross Tam's mind that a good couple of right hooks would have these wee creatures running for their lives, but then what? Back to the jungle only to be caught again or worse killed by some vicious creature.

They must have been walking for about an hour when they saw other natives approach them. They seemed extremely curious about the two captive men, the children jumped about and squealed towards Davie and Tam. It was obvious that this was the people of their village and, sure enough they were soon entering what was a large area with an oval shaped structure. It was basically a slopping roof, covering what seemed to be the living and sleeping area for the families of the village. The roof enclosed what was a huge central open area where most of the work was carried out, preparing food, cooking, sitting together, playing and making all sorts of tools and bedding.

Davie reckoned the central area was about the size of half a football field and, as he looked around figured there were at least two hundred occupants within the compound.

As they neared the inner part of the compound the strangest of sights greeted Davie and Tam, as a white man walked towards them.

"Am I seein' things Davie?" Whispered Tam, towards his friend.

He was a lean man who looked to be around 45 years old, to their surprise, he was clean shaven and wore quite worn shirt and trousers as well as a tattered Panama hat. He spoke to them in what they perceived as French, before he turned to Spanish, then to their delight, English.

"Who the fuck are you?" Was Tam's terse question towards the man.

"Charles Porteous, and you gentlemen look like two escaped convicts, yes?"

Davie was next to speak, "Your right but we didn't do anything......other than escape execution from the........".

"Hellhole!" Said Porteous cutting in.

"Ye, the very place......look, who are these people.......what are they likely to do with us?" Asked Tam.

"Probably eat you." Was Charles Porteous's terse reply.

"Oh aye, then why didn't they eat you?" Asked Davie as the natives moved them towards the top of their compound.

"Oh, they think I'm a God."

"A what!" Quizzed Tam.

"Gentlemen, if I get the opportunity, I will explain later, for now I leave you in the hands of the Yanomami people and their living area which you are within is called a Shabono."

"The Yano... what people." Said Davie as he and Tam were bound to a large upright pole stuck in the ground at the top of the Shabono. As this was being done, four elderly men and one woman approached from the roofed area of the compound and circled Tam and Davie who watched them suspiciously. They were assuming they were chiefs or leaders of these people. One of them wore a cloak, which had all sorts of items attached to it from beads to bones and feathers.

Tam nodded towards him; "Some kind o' fuckin' witchdoctor if you ask me Davie."

"Just as long as he's no the fuckin' chef Tam, we'll be ok."

Davie's remark caused Tam to snigger, "Glad you still got your sense o' humour Davie."

The native leaders mumbled amongst themselves before they turned to Porteous, who in turn turned towards Davie and Tam.

"Gentlemen, the man with the cloak is called a Tuxawa, which means chief or headman and he has instructed me that they will decide what to do with you at tonight's meal. Fortunately for you they have caught a Taper today, which will be roasted for tonight's feast. Had they not caught this beast it seems that either of you may have been the main course."

"Thank God for the .... what did you call it, a Taper?" Said Davie.

"Yes," continued Porteous, "a tasty beast quite common to the Yanomami diet, not unlike pork," continued Porteous, in his strong French accent.

Davie and Tam were made to sit at the foot of the pole they were tied to as they continued to quiz Charles Porteous about how he came to be here and how he was called a God, and they were set for the dinner table.

"You have to know gentlemen that I was …….. well, still am I suppose, a pilot of a light aircraft which flew supplies and men out to the woodcutters of the rainforest on behalf of the Brazilian Government. Sadly, I flew into a rather nasty storm and my plane came down on to the treetops not too far from here. When the Yanomami saw me glide down the rope I had thrown from my plane, that, gentlemen, is when they thought I was a God ascending from the heavens."

"And how long ago was that?" Asked Tam.

"I have been with the Yanomami for two years now and quite content I am as well, I've picked up most of their language in that time and they also gave me a young wife (he pointed to a quite pretty young woman who smiled back at him) to warm my bed at night"

"Woe woe, just a minute there, you mean you actually like it here, with these…. these……savages?" Said Tam.

"You have to understand gentlemen my life in Rio De Janeiro was very dangerous, you see I had accumulated a lot of debt to the cartels there and they were after my life……so, before I came down in the trees it was life here, or death back in Brazil."

The Spirit of St. Andrew

"So, where were you flying too before you crashed?" Came back Davie.

"I was heading north to Mexico, to do what, I don't know... who knows what life brings, I mean look at you two gentlemen, you are now like me are you not?"

Davie and Tam looked at each other before Tam answered.

"Other than us maybe going to be eaten soon, ye, I suppose there are similarities. Thing is, we were stitched up by the Savanta Police for something we definitely did not do, before we escaped by jumping into the ravine, we were about to be shot and here, we are."

"You seem like a couple of ok guys, maybe I'll have a word with the Tuxawa and see about you not, being eaten, meanwhile I'll try and get you some water you look really dehydrated." Said Charles.

"A bite to eat wouldn't go amiss either." Said Tam hopefully.

"If you're lucky, maybe tonight you'll be fed."

"By God that Charles's got it all right here Davie, plenty food, a wee woman tae himsel', probably gets served hand and foot."

"Aye, no bad Tam, no bad."

Darkness fell and the lads watched as the Yanomami prepared for their evening feast. A large communal fire was alite in the centre of the Shabona. The women were doing all the work and Davie and Tam had to admit the smell of freshly cooked food was causing them both to salivate.

Davie and Tam were surprised if not relieved to be untied, it seemed they needed the post to hang the remainder of the Taper meat from. They were not totally free though as two of the Yanomami sat behind them with spears pointing at their backs no more than a foot away.

The lads watched hungrily as the food was dished out to all around them. They were also surprised by the variety of food on their plates, or pieces of flat wood. Potatoes, sweet potatoes and sweet corn as well as other vegetables they didn't recognise.

Davie watched as, whom he thought was the elderly wife of the Tuxawa, stuffed the food into her mouth. As he did, he suddenly noticed that she seemed to be choking, probably on a piece of the meet.

She was starting to get alarmed as others of the tribe watched her choke. Some of them were becoming agitated and started to point towards Davie and Tam. It looked like they were holding them responsible for what was happening to the old woman. Porteous was trying to calm them but was starting to be pushed around as the natives grew more and more belligerent.

Davie became quite alarmed and could see something had to be done and getting away from here seemed to be the

The Spirit of St. Andrew

best alternative as he suddenly sprang to his feet. It took the guard behind him by surprise as, like everyone else he was watching the poor suffering woman.

As they sat quite near the edge of the forest Davies intention was to get away by that route and he decided he needed some sort of protection to do so and decided to grab the chocking woman around her midriff and use her as cover.

Tam sprang in behind Dave and the now desperate woman, who was turning a rather purply colour. As they backed off the tribesmen were closing in slowly with pointed spears at the ready although they were quite aware of the position of the woman.

The woman started to slit down from Davie's grasp who, in response, jerked her upwards to obtain his grip. As he jerked upwards into her abdomen the lodged piece of food suddenly shot out of her mouth followed by a huge intake of breath by the woman.

As she started to come too and realised, she was being held by one of their captives she instantly started to wriggle about and scream for assistance.

To Davie and Tams surprise the Yanomami started to kneel in front of them in obeisance. They had just saved the life of the Tuxawa's wife, and they too were now suddenly elevated to the status of Davinity.

Before they knew it, they were ushered back into the centre of the Shabono where they were sat down and given a huge platter of food to eat and fresh water to drink. The lads tucked in heartily and gorged themselves to the point of bursting.

"What the fuck did you do to that wifie Davie?" asked a delighted Tam.

"I have absolutely no idea Tam.......but I'm glad I did."

Next morning, after a great night's sleep the lads found themselves the centre of attention within the whole village. Once more food was brought to them in the form of fruit, mainly bananas and mangos. Two of the tribesmen took to Davie and Tam, they were giving them spears, blowpipes, bows and arrows and were making gestures as to how to use these various weapons.

"They want to show you how to use them." Said Charles Porteous, who had joined their company.

"It's quite an artillery they have Charles, is it all just for hunting?" Asked Tam, as he pulled on one of the bows.

"Mostly......" Said Porteous, ".... but they do have enemies within the rainforest, in particular a tribe named the Kayapo. Neighbouring tribes sometimes raid each other's Shabono's, mainly to steal women. They're all aware of the dangers of too close breading and like to get a bit of........variety, into the mix. It's only about three weeks ago that the Kayapo attacked our Shabono and took off with two young women."

"The bastards!" Snaped Tam.

"Oh, I wouldn't get to upset the villagers here are planning a return attack soon, might just get the girls back with a couple of theirs thrown in for good measure." Replied Charles.

CHAPTER 15.
VISITING.

A month had passed since Davie and Tam fell into the hands of the Yanomami. It was mid-afternoon when a knock came to the door of a house in Froghall Gardens in Aberdeen. A pretty young woman answered the door though she had a sadness about her.

"Yes......" She said to the tall thin man, "........Can I help you?"

"Yes......" He said, "….... you wouldn't happen to be Helen Harley by any chance?"

"Yes..." She replied, "......but who are you?"

"Sorry. My name is William Smythe, that's Smythe with a "Y", I've just returned recently from a country called Beldovia in South America........"

"Beldovia!" Exclaimed Mary, now looking a little upset, "My Father has just been killed in that damned country."

Smythe held up a stopping hand, "Actually Miss, he may not have been."

The Spirit of St. Andrew

"What!" Shouted Helen, before pausing, "Look Mr Smythe, perhaps you'd better come in."

"Thank you," he said as he entered. They then sat opposite each other in Helen's living room next to the fire.

Helen then reached to the mantel piece where she picked up a letter and handed it to Smythe.

"It's a telegram, from the British government, telling me that my dad had been executed by the Beldovian government for murder." Said a now tearful Helen.

"The thing is Miss Harley I was with your father the day he was due to be executed.........."

"You were? oh my God you saw my dad die?" Said Helen, her hand now across her mouth with shock.

"But that's just it Miss Harley, your father didn't die. He and his friend Thomas Goodison, made the most daring escape I have ever seen."

"Oh my God!" Exclaimed Helen, "You mean my dad's alive, but where is he.... I mean where did he escape to?"

"Into the rainforest." Replied Smythe.

"The rainforest.... what's that?"

Smythe thought for a few seconds, "Well, you'll have seen the jungle on films...?"

"Yes, in Tarzan movies, Jonny Weissmuller and all that."

"That's right, just like that, only massive. Mile upon mile of jungle, filled with cannibals and wild beasts, snakes the lot."

Again, Helen put her hand to her mouth, "Jesus, how the hell will he get from there back to hear Mr Smythe?"

"Well Miss Harley, in the little time I knew your father he came across to me as a very resilient man who had got himself out of tight spots in the past, particularly the great war, and he said that when I got back here, I was to contact you and tell you that, no matter how long it takes he will get back home."

"Well, at least I can tear up this telegram Mr Smythe....was there anything else he said?"

"There was, he asked me to get the contact address for his brother in America, he said you would have it."

"Yes, I do, but what would he want you to contact Wull about?"

" Wull......he said his brother's name was William."

Helen laughed softly, "Mr Smythe, Wull is a derivative of William in Scotland."

"Oh, I see, the Scots dialect......yes, he wanted me to contact him to tell him of his plight and ask if he would have any sway with the American government to help clear his name in Beldovia. A long shot I'm sure you'll agree, but if he were to fall into their hands again, anything that could help his cause would be of benefit."

Helen got Smythe the relevant information, they chatted for a while longer about Davies plight before Smythe left with a promise that should he hear anything relevant, he would contact Helen and let her know.

CHAPTER 16.
LIFE WITH THE YANOMAMI.

Davie and Tam were trying their very best to adapt to their now new lifestyle in the Amazon rainforest. They had now been a month with the Yanomami and were getting close to the two Yanomami men who had given them weapons when they were first treated like God's for saving the elderly woman from choking to death.

They had strange names, at least strange to Davie and Tam, Lor and Hor. Lor was slightly taller of the two and had two fingers missing on his left hand, caused he said, "By a very large stone being dropped on his hand". The two men often made Davie and Tam laugh with their antics and, because of this and their names, Davie and Tam had taken to calling them "Laurel" and "Hardy".

Laurel and Hardy were teaching the lads the ways of the jungle, how to hunt, to light fires, how to fish when they ventured to the river about two miles away. Once, when they were being taught how to use a blow pipe, Tam blew into the thing without thinking and stuck a dart in Davies backside. Fortunately, it had not been treated with poison,

The Spirit of St. Andrew

and when Davie jumped in the air, Lor suddenly impersonated him by dancing around holding his backside like it was him who had been hit. Even the little kids were in uproar at Lor antics. Davie then started to chase Lor around the Shabono causing even more uproarious laughter.

Davie and Tam were picking up a few Yanomami words here and there but were still reliant on Charles Porteous for translation. He had also let them make use of his "cut-throat" razor to shave and trim their hair. As often as not the three white men would sit and talk when they were eating.

"You two Scots seem to be taking to life here." Said Porteous.

"Well," said Davie, "were alive, whether were happy to be here is something else."

"Surly you need for nothing here gentlemen, why not be happy?"

"Need for nothing......." Said a cranky sounding Tam, ".......Jesus, maybe these natives are happy running around all but near naked but the bloody mosquitoes are bitin' at me all the time, I could kill for some mare claze".

"Claze?" Quizzed Charles.

"Sorry Charles he means clothes." Said Davie

"Oh, my dear fellow why didn't you say. I know where there are shirts about your size."

"You do........where?" Shouted Tam.

"Why, in my Plane. I transported clothing to the lumberjacks and there are shirts left over from my last trip."

"Your Plane......I thought you crashed it?" Quizzed Davie.

"Yes I did, into the tree's...it's still stuck up there."

"Can we go to it and get them.... the shirts?" Asked Tam.

"I think so, but you'd need the men here to take you....at least so far. They still think it's sacred ground and won't go close up."

"Jesus, let's go!" Exclaimed Tam, as he rose to leave.

The lads watched as Charles spoke to Laurel and Hardy about taking them. They both looked apprehensive but decided to go just if they did not have to go up close.

They'd been walking for around half an hour when they arrived at a small clearing and the natives refused to go any further. They indicated ahead to where Davie and Tam assumed the plane was, but they would go no further.

Davie and Tam wandered on. Firstly, the large Mahogany tree came into view, and as they walked around it looking upwards all the time, till finally, the aircraft was there, a Cessna NC2 single engine plane, trapped in the breech of the huge tree.

The Spirit of St. Andrew

"Jesus Davie, it's like that Linburg blokes' plane. What was it he called it, "The Spirit of St Louis"."

"Your right Tam it is a bit like it, but I think this one's a bit bigger. Look, Charles's rope's still danglin' from it."

Tam pulled on the rope, and it took his weight.

"You goin' up mate?........" Asked Davie, ".......it's a good forty feet up and that rope looks a bit....well.... ropey."

"Nae bother for me Davie." Said Tam as he started to pull himself up via the rope.

He was around halfway up when the plane suddenly jerked forward about three feet causing Tam to cry out.

"Steady ye bastard!"

When he felt it had settled, he carried on till he reached the plane. The pilot side door was still open from Charles making his decent, so Tam had no problem clambering in.

"Wow!" He went, as he gazed on the control panel and the rest of the flying controls. There were two seats at the front and storage space in behind them. He could also see that the wildlife had got to it as the seats were badly torn. No doubt Monkeys at play. Tam then started to look around for the shirts Charles had spoken about and, true to his word there they were inside a wooden box. Obviously, the box had protected the tartan woodcutter shirts from the environment and wildlife, which to Tam's delight when he unfurled one of them, it seemed the ideal size for him and Davie.

"Success!" He shouted down to his friend as he threw out a shirt towards him.

Davie caught it and put it on. Tams was a blue tartan while Davies was red, the colours of the football teams they supported. Davie enjoyed the feel of the soft material around him, not to mention the protection the shirt would give from the insect life of the rainforest.

Tam was all eyes as he took in all that was available within the plane. A fair-sized toolbox with tools was the next thing he lowered via the rope to Davie below. He then noticed what he was sure was an inflatable dingy, and beside it a pump for blowing it up.

"Handy," He thought as he lowered it as well, although when he did move it, he noticed some damage in parts caused by wildlife.

Tam's next find caused his eyes to widen as he opened the glove-type compartment of the panel dashboard.

"I'll keep you to myself," He mumbled softly, as he put the item in his trouser pocket.

"Right, that's its Davie, I'm comin' down now."

Slowly, Tam slid down the rope but was in for a shock. Suddenly, about halfway down the rope snapped leaving Tam to fall the last 10 yards or so to the rainforest floor. Fortunately, it was thick with leaves which helped cushion his fall.

"You ok Tam?" Asked Davie, as he helped Tam to his feet.

"Aye fine...." Answered Tam, as he looked up to where he had fallen from and saw the remains of the rope dangling about thirty feet above him, "......nobody goin' up there again, that's for sure."

"Aye, yer right big man, still, the rope could've broken just as you left the plane, then you'd of got a right clatter!"

A reception awaited the lads back at the Shabono as the children all seemed to want to touch Davie and Tams newfound shirts. Davie had his mind set on something else though. He soon had the foot pump fixed up to the dingy to find out just how badly damaged it was. The boat itself was in sections, two main sections down the middle, a half moon one at the top and a smaller one at the rear end. Sadly, only the two central ones seemed to hold the air, while the end ones were badly damaged.

"Shit!" Exclaimed Davie, as he took a kick at the punctured ends.

This caused the onlooking Charles to smirk, "What? You didn't think this small dingy would get you out of here, did you?"

"Maybe." Snarled Davie, who was now joined by Tam as well.

The Spirit of St. Andrew

"Jesus..." continued Davie, as he looked on at their smiling sarcasm, "......don't either of you two want to get to hell out of this God forsaken place?"

"Where the hell too, Davie?" Asked Charles.

"Home! For fuck's sake, home!" He snarled back.

"Well, Davie, it won't be in that." Said Charles, pointing to the dingy.

"Ok smarty pants, just how in the hell would you suggest we get to hell out o' this place?"

"My friend, I've told you before, I have no desire to leave here, but if I were to.... yes....it would be by the river, after all, the one closest to us does seem to flow in a south easterly direction but you are talking about a journey of at least 50 to 75 miles of God knows what kind of waters.... rapids, waterfalls, rocks, Pirahna's....".

"What the hell are Piranhas?" Asked Tam.

"Killer fish. Fish that can eat a man down to the bone in a matter of seconds."

"What about that bloody plane of yours?" Asked Davie changing the subject slightly.

Porteous shrugged his shoulders, "Well, apart from being stuck on the top of a tree and probably in need of a new engine, the main problem after you got all that sorted is that you need about 200 yards of runway for it to take off, my friend."

The Spirit of St. Andrew

"Wow......." said Tam, his tongue firmly in his cheek, "that's about two football fields long. Still, we could always get in touch with the lads at the "Hellhole" and ask for a loan o' one o' their chainsaw things and clear the way!"

"Oh aye, very funny Goodison."

All three than had a chuckled at Tam's suggestion.

As they sat talking the three lads were approached by a group of about ten of the Yanomami including Laurel and Hardy. They spoke to Charles before they all set off towards the undergrowth.

"What are they up to Charles?" Asked Davie.

"Remember how I told you this village had been raided by the Kayapo tribe and taken two of their young women. It would seem they are off to try and get them back and maybe add a couple."

"Wow, how long will that take?" Asked Davie.

"Nearly a day there and about the same back, if all goes well."

That same night there was quite a storm got up. Davie was tossing around on his sleeping bench, the noise of the wind and thunder reminding him only too well of the nights in the trenches of France.

Come morning Davie rose early as he was fed up with tossing around on his bed. As he left the sheltered area of the Shabono he was aware that the weather had settled, when he saw some of the other native men who were still here getting ready for the mornings hunt. These men knew that the wildlife can be quite disorientated when the weather is as wild as it was last night.

Davie picked up on their excitement and indicated to them that he wanted to come along, to which they agreed. Davie recognised the direction they had taken; it was the same way they went when they looked for Charles Porteous plane.

They were well into the rainforest and had already brought down two monkeys with blow pipes. Davie had been well warned not to touch the tips of the darts used to bring down their prey. They were tinted with the venom found on the backs of poison dart frogs and could stun or even kill their prey as well as humans.

They had been away for well over an hour when two of the men came to Davie urging him to follow them. Davie soon realised they were heading to where Charles's plane was and sure enough about twenty yards to where it was, Davie was urged to go forward himself and see.

To Davie's astonishment Charles Cessna plane had been blown from the treetops and was lying slightly tilted on the ground due to one of the wheels being broken. The Yanomami stayed well back as Davie took a close look at the damage. He looked up the tree from where it had come and noticed the large branch that had been holding it had snapped, allowing the plane to fall. The tail area and backward half was still free of the ground and in good condition.

On the way back to the Shabono, Davies mind was in overdrive. His main, initial thought, was always, could this thing be made to fly again? He and Tam were quite mechanically minded, what was so wrong with the engine that it couldn't be fixed? While out hunting with the Yanomami he'd came on some large clearings of previous settlements, and he thought of what they had done at the "Hellhole" to get planes in and out.

When they arrived back at the Shabono, Davie was quick to gather Charles and Tam together to tell them what he had found, and what he was thinking.

"Davie," Said Tam right away, "at the "Hellhole" they brought in chainsaws and big tools as well as a batch of prisoners to work on a runway........"

Charles then cut in, "Never mind all that," He said, "when I knew the plane was coming down, I was aware of how low I was on fuel. The nearest supply was around fifty miles away and I had just about enough to get there. Sadly, what was left has surly evaporated or leaked away over the time it has been stuck up that tree."

"What!" Exclaimed Davie, "You mean there's no a drop o' fuel in that thing?"

"Yes, and there's certainly none to be got around here."

"Fuck!" Shouted Davie.

"Davie, for God's sake man, yer livin' in a dream world...." Said Tam, "......think about it. Yer lookin' for a non-existent runway to fly a busted plane that has no fuel and would need transported through the jungle to wherever this non-existent runway is going to be.... wake up man." Tam continued, "Look mate if you must get away fae here why don't you do what they do in the movies and build a raft or something."

"Jesus Tam, do ye no think ah've thought oh that, but ah've looked ah aroond this place, the Yanomami have use up most o' the fallen wood tae prop up their Shabono and keep their fires goin', and there's a distinct lack o' good cuttin' tools like saws and axes tae dae the work, and all that is before a think aboot what am goin' tae tie the bloody wood together we."

The lad's conversation was suddenly disturbed by the return of the raiding party that had left the previous morning and they did not look at all happy. They did have the two women who had been taken before, though one of them seemed a little unhappy to be back as she struggled with the native pulling her along. What soon became apparent though, was that Lor was not with them. Hor was giving Charles all the information which he soon passed on to Davie and Tam.

"Well gentlemen, the upshot is that poor Lor was captured by the Kayapo during the raid and the rest of them just got away by the skin of their teeth."

"Jesus..." Said Tam, ".... what the hell will happen to him?"

"More than likely the Kayapo with use him for a celebratory feast tonight." Was Charles terse reply.

"Barbaric bastards......." said Davie, "....is there nothing that can be done."

"Well....." Said Charles, ".... Hor here wants to go back and get his brother, but all the other men are exhausted. They've been running all night that's why there back so soon."

Davie and Tam looked at each other before Davie spoke, "Tell Hor we'll go with him to get Laural......elm, Lor."

Hor's face lit up as he went to collect weapons for Davie and Tam who quickly grabbed some food to eat before setting off. Hor soon returned with one other man who had decided to go with them.

Charles stopped Davie and Tam just before they left.

"Listen lads, I've talked to some of the Yanomami who came back with Hor, and they said that the Kayapo have a new chief, and he seems quite fierce. Unusually tall for a native of the rainforest about my height the men said and I'm 5foot 9 inches. They heard them call his name, Maboosh, and he looked very angry that they had managed to get away from him, so, be careful gentlemen."

Hor was setting a fair pace despite being tired from the raid earlier. They knew they had to get there before the

Kayapo started feasting. Davie and Tam were feeling the pace but kept up. They were aware of the severity of the situation and didn't want to be the ones that would cause a hold up.

They were all pleased to arrive before darkness feel. They stopped around 200 yards short of the Kayapo Shabono, where they decided to rest until it fell dark.

Now dark enough, the four men crept as close to the Shabono as they dare. As they peered through the undergrowth, they could see that preparations were being made for the night's festivities. A large central fire was already well aflame.

It was then that Hor prodded Davie and signalled to him that he could see Lor at the edge of the Shabono, tied to a post just as Davie and Tam had been when they were captured by the Yanomami. Two Kayapo natives sat guard beside him facing the festivity preparations, making Davie realise that someone would have to get in behind Lor to cut him loose.

Tam volunteered and was soon crawling along the ground to where Lor was tied. There were drums beating as the Kayapo started to work themselves up into a frenzy for the coming feast. Tam was now in behind Lor, Tam tapped on his arm. Lor immediately spun his head around and saw Tam who was holding his finger over his mouth to indicate to Lor not to make a sound as he started to cut the rope that bound Lor who was in a sitting position, his hands tied behind the pole.

The Spirit of St. Andrew

The two guards were watching the proceedings within the Shabono, quite confident that the prisoner was going nowhere. Lor slowly started to move, firstly by raising his feet, then twisting around, before slowly moving towards Tam. As soon as he was level with Tam, Lor sprang to his feet and along with Tam, started to run.

One of the guards caught site of Lor out of the corner of his eye and immediately gave out a roar. All hell seemed to break loose as Kayapo natives started darting about all over the place.

Tam and Lor were now sprinting through the undergrowth towards Davie, Hor, and the other Yanomami native. It was dark and hard to see where they were going. That was when Davie and Hor started shouting to the two men what direction to take. As they ran towards the sound, they were both very aware that the two guards were closing in rapidly. Further back they were also aware of more of the Kayapo following with burning torches held above their heads.

Ahead of Tam, Davie and the other two were now also starting to run through the undergrowth, and was shouting, "Come on.... come on!"

Tam, with Lor hard on his heals was aware that the chasing guards were almost upon them and got quite a shock when a spear flew past his right ear.

"Fuckin' hell!" He shouted out as he felt his throat burn with the extreme breathing.

Then disaster, when Lor fell over some branch or another and spread eagled behind Tam who immediately pulled up and turned just in time to see one of the guards, spear raised, ready to plunge his weapon into Lor.

Incredibly everyone was suddenly terrified by the loudest of bangs that only Davie recognised. To him it was obviously a gunshot which brought him to a sudden halt. He instantly headed to where the shot came from and soon saw Tam standing pointing a pistol at the other Kayapo native who was looking at his fellow Kayapo writhing on the ground holding his thigh. The native seemed almost paralysed with fear as he stood, spear raised looking at Tam. He was a tall, fierce looking fellow, probably the one that was called Maboosh they had been told about. He certainly was an imposing looking character but didn't exactly scare Tam. Tam didn't hesitate and fired another round into the air which was enough to send even Maboosh scampering off in terror.

"Where the fuck did you get that?" Shouted Davie as he arrived at Tam.

"From Porteous's plane......" Was Tam's terse reply, ".......didn't know if it would work though, but, thank fuck that it did."

"Right..." said Davie, ".... let's get tae fuck oot o' here before the whole village is on us."

"I don't know Davie, somehow I think what just happened will have scared the bejesus out o' them." Replied Tam.

Back at the Shabono the returning raiders were treated like royalty as the children cheered and the men all patted Davie Tam and the other two natives on their backs.

That night around the feast fire two young women were brought forward to Davie and Tam, it was the two brought back by the earlier raid. Davie and Tam had curious looks on their faces as the Tuxawa spoke to Charles, looking at the lads as he did.

"Something's up Davie." Whispered Tam to his friend.

"Aye, and I've an idea what......." Replied Davie, a look of concern on his face, "...and it's got something to do with these women, mate."

Tam's face lit up, "What, you mean the same as Charlie boy, were to get a woman each.....Ho Ho!"

Sure enough, Charles approached the lads with the two, quite attractive, young women, certainly no more than 20 years old, "these are for you gentlemen for your courage and bravery......enjoy!"

One of the women immediately went towards Tam, a large smile on her face and seemingly quite happy with the arrangement.

"Tam, this canny be right.......can it?"

"Davie, have you never heard the expression, you don't look a gift horse in the mouth." said Tam, putting his arm around his new companion, who grinned broadly up to Tam as he did.

Davie's, woman, didn't seem quite so pleased with the pairing and stood with a "hangdog" look about her.

That night Tam kept most of the Shabono occupants awake with his grunts and groans as he took full advantage of his new young partner, who in turn seemed to be enjoying the occasion as well. Davie, on the other hand, seemed at a loss as to what to do with the situation, although not keen on what was happening, he could see the young woman was not at all "up for it" either. She mumbled away at Davie, and there was only one word he was picking up on throughout all her rambling, and that was "Maboosh".

To Davie's mind, it didn't take a genius to work out that while held captive the girl had been matched up with the big Kayapo chief, and she was smitten. He recalled her not being so happy at being brought back by the raiding party.

That night the last thing Davie remembered before falling asleep was the young woman still weeping quietly to herself. Davie never laid a finger on her.

Davie was alone when he woke up and seeing the girl wasn't there assumed she had just risen early. After looking around the place for a while it soon became apparent to Davie that his newly assigned female "gift", was nowhere to be found.

"She's gone back to Maboosh......." said Charles, as he approached Davie, "........the elders just told me they worked hard trying to get her to forget about him but, it seemed she was infatuated by the big Kayapo."

"Well," Said Davie, "I can't exactly say I'm heartbroken........wasn't at all keen on the whole setup anyway."

Tam emerged from the Shabono with his new woman by his side.

"What's up Davie.......where's yer burd?"

"Gone!" Said Davie.

"Gone?............gone where?" Asked Tam, with a shrug of his shoulders.

"She took of this morning back to the Kayapo. It seemed she was Maboosh's woman." Said Charles.

"Augh Davie, you must be heartbroken mate Maboosh must've had a bigger dick than you." Teased Tam.

"Shut yer puss Tam, God ye can be a right pain in the arse sometimes." snapped Davie.

"Oooh touchy." Said Tam, just to keep it going, "Still, me and Looma here, got on great last night Davie......ah think it might be love."

The Spirit of St. Andrew

"Away and no talk a lot oh shite Tam......Love for fuck sake!"

"Hey....what's wrong we that?" Snaped back Tam, his tongue firmly in his cheek.

Davie was starting to lose his rag with his mate, "What's wrong we it, are you fuckin' mad. I mean, what's the plan Tam, are you going to settle down here, have a few bairns, build yer ain Shabono, become the fuckin' chief, ye daft bastard!"

"Maybe!" Retorted Tam, "and what the fuck are you goin' tae dae, rebuild a busted aeroplane, dig oot a runway 200 yards long, make fuckin' petrol oot o' banana juice, and fly away back tae Aiberdeen.......you're, the daft bastard!"

"Enough!" Shouted Charles, as he looked to the heavens, "God you Scot's, you would fight with your own fucking shadows."

"If only......" continued Davie, "......this God forsaken dark hole o' a place disnae even give ye a shadow. All ye get is pouring fuckin' rain, bitten to death by mossies' and listenin' tae yer mate shaggin' the hale night."

"Well at least yer alive ye miserable bugger." Came back Tam.

"Oh aye, yer right Tam, am alive ok, but am I really livin'?"

"Ok, ok, you two," Interrupted a now frustrated Charles, "You are not going to solve anything shouting back and forth at each other. Listen, Davie, I think you really do need to work on a plan to get yourself to hell out of here and on your way home.........how you are going to do that though, I have no idea I'm afraid."

"It's funny you should say that Charlie, because I have been planning something. I still think I can get away from here using the plane." Said Davie.

"Awe for God's sake Davie......." went Tam, looking to the heavens.

"Hold on, just hear me out. Charlie, what is the body o' your plane made from?" Asked Davie.

"I believe it's a very light Tin material, why?" He asked.

"Right, hear me out." Said Davie as he crouched down where the other two were sitting. "The back end of your plane is fairly big and hollow, right?"

"Yes, why?"

"Ok, I noticed all the tools you had in the toolbox we took from your plane, hacksaw, metal snips, hammers, plyers, brace and bits, spanners even a roll of solder and a soldering bolt."

"Yes, so?"

"So, if we could cut the back of the plan away from the rest of it, I believe we could shape it into a boat and get away via the bloody river!"

The other two fell silent as they stared at each other before Charles spoke.

"Davie, I see where you're coming from, but you have to understand about buoyancy in the water......."

"Agh...." Davie cut in, "......I thought about that and your right it probably would tip over or capsize or whatever you call it, but......"

"But what!" Snapped an annoyed Tam.

"What if we took the two sides of the inflatable dingy and fixed one to either side of the boat....Vaala.....buoyancy!" Said a smug looking Davie with his hands held out to the side and a broad grin across his face.

Once again, silence, as Charles and Tam looked at each other a little stunned.

"Now...." continued Davie, "......I know what you're both thinking......."

"You do?" Interrupted Charles.

"Yes......" went Davie, "You're thinking if we cut the back off, there's going to be a great gaping hole at the end away from the tail......yes?"

"There is?"

"Yes, there is.... but we then cut the top part of the tail away, this should be a nice big sheet of your tin or whatever it is, and we fix it over the open space. That of course will be the back of the boat, with the tail end turned to make the helm, brilliant...no?"

Again, a long stare from the other two before Tam broke the silence, "And just where are ye goin' tae dae a this, boat building?"

"Right here." Was Davies quick retort, before he continued, "We go to the plane, cut out the back end like I said, then carry it back here......I mean it's light material, I reckon four men will carry it using Charlie's rope. The tools are all here as well as the work force."

"But the Yanomami won't go near the plane Davie." Said Charles.

"I thought of that, and that is where I want you to use your powers of persuasion to get them involved......I mean they owe us for going on the raid with them, no?"

Davie then got up to go.

"Where ye goin' Dave?" asked Tam.

"For a much-needed bath." Was Davies strange reply.

"A bath.... where...how?"

"In the big pool at the stream........guess what I found in Charlie's plane?"

Davie then held up a cube shaped red block the size of the palm of his hand.

The Spirit of St. Andrew

"Soap.... you found soap." Said Tam excitedly, as he stood up.

"Yip." Replied Davie, "And I'm off to borrow Charlie's razor as well."

"Hold on Davie, I'm commin' we ye."

Charles talked to the Yanomami, telling them that the spirit around the plane had been lifted since Tam and Davie went into the plane, and that no one could be cursed. He also used Davies persuasive line about returning the favour he had done for them. Lor and Hor didn't hesitate and persuaded a couple of others to join in as well.

Davie and Tam were soon back.

"My God, you two smell and look a lot fresher." Said Charles.

"Aye...." said Tam, ".... he scrubbed my back, and I scrubbed his."

"That's right...." continued Davie, ".......and I shaved his puss and he shaved mine."

"Well," went Charles, "very lovey-dovey."

Charles went on to tell the lads that the Yanomami were prepared to help with the plane and before long they were all on their way.

So soft was the metal framing that it didn't take long with the hacksaw blades to cut the back of the plane away from

The Spirit of St. Andrew

the rest. A cheer went up when it fell to the ground ready for transporting. Charles had quite a length of rope within the plane and soon two slings were attached around the back and the front.

Davie and Tam were at each side of the front part, thought to be the heaviest, with Laurel and Hardy at the back.

"One, two, three, lift!" shouted Davie, and with unexpected ease, the four lifted the potential boat off the ground and were soon on their way with Charles and the other two Yanomami following on carrying the tools. Although there was a small wheel at the back of the plane, the lads found it too small as it continually caught up in the thick leaves, it turned out to be easier to lift.

It seemed like everyone in the village leant a hand as the craft was slowly knocked into shape. Every nut and bolt they could find was taken from the remainder of the plane and used to bolt the piece taken from the top to be placed across the gaping hole at what would become the back of the boat. To waterproof it, Davie soldered all the way around the join and gave a cheer when he finished, holding a piece of solder wire about an inch long in the air to show how tight the whole operation was.

Pieces of wood were place inside and fixed for the passengers and rower to sit on. A hole was cut in the back for a wooden rudder to be place through. The back of the plane, which was now the front of the boat, had the top piece of the plane tail removed as well as the side flaps, but the rest of the top was left after the large piece had been taken. The Idea was that this might be a handy cove for keeping the food dry and for a small cover at night to crawl into should it be raining.

Sap from rubber trees was used to help fix the two rubber dingy sides to the craft. The cord attached to the dingy was also used to help bolster the inflatable parts to the sides. The lowest part of the boat was now at the front, so it was here that they attached the inflated parts at either side.

Tam, with the help of his new companion Looma, had made a sort of paint out of the sap as well. They had mixed it with animal blood to brighten the colour. Tam kept a cover over what he was painting along the side and told everyone it would be revealed at the launch.

Around two weeks had passed, and the boat was nearing completion. It was while they were adding finishing touches one afternoon that the days hunting party returned, and they were carrying something that was not their usual catch. It was the slightly decomposed body of the young woman who had fled the night she was given to Davie.

After the hunters had consulted with Charles, he told the lads that it seemed she must have taken a wrong turning and got herself a bit lost but crucially, they found marks of a snake bite on the calf of her leg.

"Jesus Harley if you'd just shown her a bit of affection, she might not have left." Said Tam, a slight anger in his voice.

"What did you just say...?" Growled Davie, as he turned to make eye contact with Tam.

"You heard." Was Tams response.

That was it for Davie as he made a grab for Tam. Almost immediately the two were rolling around the ground trying to hit each other with blows but having little success. Before the fight went much further, Lor and Hor, along with Charles were pulling the two men apart. The two stood glowering at each other as the two Yanomami men stood between them.

"It's time you learned Goodison that there's mare tae life than shaggin'." Shouted Davie.

"Oh aye, and how the fuck would you ken, conciderin' ye never dae any, ye poofy bastard."

That set Davie off again as he tried to break free of Hor and Lor, but they kept him back.

"Gentlemen, gentlemen please, for God's sake.......look, it was no one's fault the girl died......" said Charles, still holding out his hands to keep them apart, ".........she was hell bent on getting back to Maboosh no matter what Davie had done.......right.......Tam, you need to apologise."

"What........." Was Tams astonished reply," ".......Will I fuck!"

The Spirit of St. Andrew

"Look, just forget it." Said Davie, as he brushed Hor's hand aside and walked off to the Shabono.

Tam flatly refused to help on the boat after that. He spent most of his days just wandering around with Looma on his arm.

While Davie worked on the craft the piece of animal hide Tam had covering his paint work fell off. There it was for all to see, "The Spirit of St Andrew".

Davie had a wry smile when he saw it, he remembered Tam mention Charles Linburg and the "Spirit of St Louis", how appropriate that for two Scot's, he should name it after their patron saint.

That night at mealtime Davie went over and sat beside Tam and Looma.

"I like the name." Was Davie's opening line to try and break the ice.

"The name?" Went Tam, tilting his head back to look into Davies eyes.

"Aye, "The Spirit of St Andrew". Said Davie.

"Oh aye, right, you werny meant tae see that till launch day." Said Tam, who then went on, "Look Davie, Charles was right, I do owe you an apology, I was bang out of order sayin' what I said."

Davie taped Tam's knee with his hand, "Forget it mate. Maybe in a small way you were right, she may have stayed.......thing is......we'll never know."

Tam quickly changed the subject, "So, yer wee boats aboot ready tae launch."

"Aye," Said Davie, "another couple o' day's ah should think........are you comin'?"

"Naw, I'm fine here." He said as he pulled Looma into himself.

"Surely you dinny mean that Tam, I mean, do ye no miss the comforts o' life back home man, bacon and egg for breakfast, mince and tatties and peas for dinner, a warm soft bed we nae mossies' eatin' away at ye. No tae mention Saturday afternoon at the match, watchin' the Dee getting' thrashed fae the Don's."

"Ye were dain' fine till that last bit Davie, for ye ken fine Dundee would thump yer Aberdeen shite." Sniped Tam.

"All kiddin' aside Tam, you've got tae realise that this is probably the only chance in the rest o' yer life that you'll be able tae get away fae this God forsaken place......I mean the rest o' yer life."

Tam thought for a while, "Aye, yer probably right in what you say Davie.......do you remember ah told ye aboot Kathleen...ye know, durin' the Great War."

"Aye, yer first love.... she died."

"Aye, well, the thing is, that was the only time a woman ever loved me, oh ah ken ah've been we loads oh dames in different ports ah ower the world, but none o' them meant anythin' tae me, not after Kathleen." Said Tam, who then hesitated.

"Aye, and……." Quizzed Davie.

"See this wee lassie here……." said Tam, pointing at Looma, "…. she is daft on me and am fond o' her…….that's why ah canny go. I have a chance tae settle here."

"Jesus Tam, your fuckin' serious, aren't ye?" Said a rather shocked Davie.

"Never been more serious in my life."

"So, your goin' tae be happy here huntin' fuckin' monkeys and Tapers and raisin' we half breeds and fightin' the Kayapo and shitin' in the woods and wipin' yer arse we dead leaves?" Was Davies terse reply.

"Now Davie…." Said Tam, holding up a stopping hand, "……I can see you startin' tae get upset and that is only goin' tae lead tae mare conflict between the two o' us, so, I think we better just stop there". Davie said no more.

CHAPTER 17.
GOODBYE TO THE YANOMAMI.

Along with a couple of the Yanomami, Davie was putting the finishing touches to the "Spirit of St Andrew" himself, as Tam sat with Looma, watching.

It was then that Charles came over to Tam and asked if he could have a word. Tam indicated for Charles to sit beside him before he spoke.

"Tam, now I know it's none of my business but............"

Tam immediately cut in, "You know Charlie, it really worries me when people start a conversation like that, because it's bound to be the case that it is, none of their business."

Charles smiled softly but carried on anyway, "Oh I think your right my friend, but I'm going to say this anyway. Are you certain you're going to watch Davie float away on his own after all you two have been through together?"

"I'm makin' a new life here Charlie, me and Looma." Answered Tam quietly, yet not all that convincingly, thought Charles.

Charles tried another tactic, "Davie's desperate to leave Tam, and he is going to have one hell of a job navigating that craft himself, especially when he hits rough waters, rowing and steering at the same time, damned near imposable"

Tam just stared out, watching Davie work, "He's a tough cookie is Davie....he'll find a way."

"Oh, I'm sure he will, but it'll be a damned sight easier with a co-pilot, don't you think?" Asked Charles, still prodding.

Tam then slowly turned and stared into Charles's eyes, "Charlie, yer startin' tae get on my tit's now, I think you better give it a wee rest."

Charles got the message and quickly held up a stopping hand, "Pardon, my friend, I meant no offence."

"None taken." Answered Tam, as Charles got up to leave.

Tam spent the rest of that day mopping around, truth be told he was caught in the arms of a dilemma. Was he really prepared to stand by and watch his friend leave on his own. This was the man who had been his true friend for nye on 20 years. He's helped Davie through the toughest times of his life, surviving the Great War together, helping him hold it together when he lost the love of his life, Jean. They'd sailed the seven seas together, got themselves in and out of scrapes that were sometimes life threatening. Could he just watch him float out of his life for ever, and it most certainly would be forever.

Davie turned his head when he heard Tam shout Charles back. He watches as he sat Charles down between himself and Looma and started to talk. It seemed by the body language that Tam wanted something translated to Looma. The two lads had, in the months they had been in the rainforest, picked up bits of Yanomami speak here and there, but not enough to hold a full-blown conversation.

That night around the Shabono central fire Davie got Charles to announce that he would be grateful for their help in taking the boat to the river tomorrow and that this would be his last night with them.

A mumble went around the camp as some of the Yanomami came over and patted Davie on the back as if to say good luck.

After things had quietened down Davie got a surprise when Tam and Looma (now his constant shadow) came and sat by him.

"So, Davie, yer of the morn, eh?" Said Tam.

"Aye ah am, and your determined to stay?" Replied Davie.

"Well, that's what ah came ower tae speak tae ye aboot........"

The Spirit of St. Andrew

Davie cut in, "What?...Yer goin'?"

"Aye, ah am, and so is Looma." Was Tam's shock reply.

"What!" Shouted Davie, "Are ye aff yer fuckin' heed."

Tam then took exception to Davie terse reply as he went to get up and go, "Right if that's yer attitude, forget it."

Davie pulled at Tam's arm to sit back down, "Ok Tam, but have you really thought this through, I mean, I think it would be really hard for you to survive here, but Looma, trying to live in Scotland, Jesus, Tam, think aboot it. Could ye see her walkin' doon the Hilltoon we 'er tits hingin' oot and a couple o' wee half breeds at 'er side. She'd get torn tae shreds by the locals, maybe no' physically, but certainly verbally."

"Well Davie, that's a pretty damning opinion ye have o' my fellow Dundonians." Replied Tam.

"Don't kid yersel' Tam, every society has there good and there bad within it, aye, even Aiberdeen."

Tam had to smile, "Anyway Davie, when ah get Looma back the first thing I'll do is buy her a beautiful blue dress. Ye know, Dundee's colours, she'll blend right in."

"That is a bloody shame Tam, how could ye dae that tae the poor lassie......, an' mare tae the point, what aboot yer bairns, they'll be runnin' the backies o' Dundee chasin' a the fuckin' stray cats and dogs we spears." Said Davie with a laugh.

Tam had to join in before he said, "Ok Davie, enough, anyway, they'll be playin' footie for the dark blues."

"Right, "Said Davie, "We had better get some mare food into that boat, enough for another two passengers it would seem."

Tam left and was immediately replaced by Charles, or Charlie as the lads had taken to calling him. Davie imparted the news to him that both Tam and Looma were to go with him.

"Wow," Said Charles, "that's quite a crew you'll have."

"You know Charlie, I'm sorry, but it never entered my head to ask you if you wanted to come with us......you know......get to hell out of here.... you'll be welcome after all you've done for us."

Charles held up a stopping hand, "Thank you my friend, but not only am I content here, but I think your small craft would be a little overcrowded."

"Sorry Charlie but I worry about you." Replied Davie.

"Why should you worry my friend, I have all I need here." Said Charles.

Davie lowered his head and shook it slowly from side to side, "It's just that I look at your clothes and, well, to say the least, there falling off you......what the fuck are you going to do when they actually just, disintegrate?"

Charles smiled then said, "Then, I shall go native, I'll wear the attire of the Yanomami."

Charles continued, "Anyway Davie I have two reasons for coming over. The first is to give you this."

Charles held out what looked to Davie like a gun in a holster.

"It's a flare pistol, sad to say there is only the one flare with it. We were issued them the same time they gave us the dingy, in case I ever came down in the ocean. You just pull back the hammer, aim it in the air, pull the trigger and….Valla".

"Brilliant." Said Davie as he strapped the holster around his waist.

Charles continued, "The other thing I wanted to ask was, what kind of plan do you have for your journey?"

Davie thought for a second, "My plan is to follow the river as far as I can, hopefully to Brazil." Replied Davie.

"Yes, certainly, from what I remember of flying over this area I seem to recall the river flows in south to south-easterly direction eventually joining the great river Amazon."

"God willing we'll get that far, hopefully make land in Brazil and give ourselves over to the authorities, then the British embassy and from there, home." Said Davie with a broad smile.

Charles smiled then tilted his head with a wink, "Sounds fine Davie, but you must not underestimate the power of the Amazon River. It is huge, the largest river in the world and it could sweep you right out into the Atlantic if you do not make land very quickly."

"I'll certainly keep that in mind Charlie, but what about the river I'm about to take on first?" Asked Davie.

"From what I recall it is for the best part fairly calm, but there are waterfalls and some strong rapids on the way down, that's why I'm happier for you that you now have help on board with you."

"Sounds like a real challenge all the same Charlie." Replied Davie, as Charles continued.

"There is of course another small problem......"

"Oh aye, and what's that?"

"The damned natives. The Yanomami will tell you; there is one very fierce tribe about a day and a half's journey down the river, they're called the Huaorani, very cannibalistic in their nature and not known for showing mercy to anyone. The Yanomami are all quite afraid of them and are grateful for the distance between them, they very rarely venture this far upriver but have in the past......that's how they know of them"

"Thanks for that Charlie, I now know I'll sleep well during the nights down river." Said Davie with wry smile.

The Spirit of St. Andrew

"Well, try to stay on the water.... you have your anchor stone on board, best use it at night." Said Charles.

The next morning was warm and as usual humid, as the whole Shabono rose early to see of Davie, Tam and Looma.

The Yanonami men were happy to take the weight of the boat and carry it the two miles to the river. Davie and Tam went ahead, cutting at the undergrowth to help clear a way through to the river. The natives shared the load taking turns as men grew tired.

When they finally arrived at the river, there was some apprehension as the boat was lowered into the water, they had tested for leeks but with all the pressures on the boat working its way through the undergrowth, there was concern that some damage may have occurred.

A cheer went up when Davie announced that all was well. The "Spirit of St Andrew" sat proudly in the river at least one foot clear of the water with the crew on board. All that remained to do was load on the food, animal skins for night covers, all of Charles rope from the plane and there was quite a lot, at least 100ft.

There was also a large stone placed at the back, which Charles had talked to Davie about. This would act as an anchor while they rested at night, not as heavy as they couldn't lift, yet not as light as allow the boat to drag it along the riverbed. There were hugs and tears and much waving of hands as the trio pulled away from the shore.

The Spirit of St. Andrew

Davie and Tam certain they were taking their last look upon the Yanomami people.

CHAPTER 18.
LIFE ON THE RIVER.

The "Spirit of St Andrew" was floating gracefully along. The river was continually around fifty feet wide so far. Davie was at the rear holding the rudder, while Tam sat in the middle working the oars. There wasn't much rowing needed as the river current drove the craft on. Looma sat at the front of the boat smiling up to Tam as he sang them on their way.

"Oh the life on the ocean wave, tar-ar-ar-ar-ar-ar-ra-rah".

"Jesus, you're some chanter Tam." said Davie with his hands over his ears.

"The voice of an angel Davie boy, the voice of an angel." Said Tam, just as Looma started to hum the tune, "He-he, a duet we Looma, gone yersels."

Suddenly Davie called for quiet, "Shshsh," he went.

"What is it?" Asked Tam, turning to his friend.

"Don't you hear that........sounds like rushing water up ahead." Said Davie, who had noticed that the river had been slowly narrowing.

"God yer right Davie, looks like a waterfall up ahead, look the water just disappears.........better pull into the side and have a look mate."

With both the oars and the rudder they manipulated the boat to the side, just short of the rushing water which they felt wanted to pull the boat onwards over the edge. They tied it to a large stone, of which there were many staggered along the edge of the fall. Looma stayed beside the boat as the two lads went to investigate. They were soon at the side of the edge of the fall and were looking down.

They had to shout to each other to be heard above the sound of the rushing water.

"That looks around thirty feet down Davie, what do you suggest?"

"We can't just let the boat go over, she could break up, I think we're going to have to lower her down to that ledge at the side of the fall."

"Aye, ok, but what about us, am no jumpin', no again?"

"We'll go down on the rope, at the side here."

"And what about Looma, she won't manage the rope Davie."

"She will if we lower her, bring her over, I'll ready the rope."

Tam brought a rather reluctant looking Looma over to where Davie was waiting to lower her over. The two fixed the rope around her upper torso, told her to hang on to the rope, whereupon they started to lower her over.

Looma was terrified as she continually called out Tam's name. He in turn was trying to reassure her as she went further and further down. It was all going well when, as Looma was around ten feet from the bottom, Charlies damned rope broke, sending Looma tumbling down the last ten feet.

Things looked ok as she landed on her feet and rolled over. As she landed, she instantly grabbed at her ankle and writhed in pain.

"Jesus, she's broken her ankle!" Shouted Tam.

"Maybe just sprained." Hoped Davie, as he pulled the remaining rope up to them.

"Right Tam we've got to get the boat and it's gear down next." Said Davie, who continued, "We'll double the rope though.... dinny want the fuckin' thing brakin' again."

They unloaded the boat of their food and cover skins and the boat was over the edge, as it neared the bottom, Tam shouted to Looma as best he could to make her understand, that she should try to guide the boat out level on to the rocks, which amazingly the girl managed to do.

"Right Tam, you are next, then I'll lower the stuff to you, we'll keep it double, just to be safe." Said Davie.

"Hold up...." said Tam, "......how in the hell are you going to get down and the rope as well?"

"I'll do a hitch-loop around this stone and pull it around once am down.... come on, let's go." Insisted Davie.

They got the other items down after Tam. It was then Davie caught site out of the corner of his eye, four natives coming down the same side of the river towards them and they were pointing towards Davie and Tam.

"A fuckin' Kayapo hunting party!" He mumbled to himself, "And they don't really like us."

Tam was at the bottom and after he saw that Looma was not too badly injured, and had made safe the rest of their cargo, he looked up to see if Davie was coming, but there was no sign. He got an even bigger shock when the whole rope fell at his feet, "what the fuck is Davie up to", thought Tam.

Suddenly, without warning he saw the figure of his pal float through the air as he jumped into the pool at the foot of the fall.

"What the ......" Shouted Tam as he waited for his friend to surface. Tam gazed into the bubbling foam at the foot of the fall in search of Davie who suddenly appeared holding out a hand for Tam to help pull him up.

"What the fuck did ye dae that for ye stupid cunt!" Went Tam as he pulled him up.

A breathless Davie just pointed up to the top of where he had just jumped from. Tam looked up and was shocked to see the four Kayapo looking down on them.

As quickly as they could, they got everything and everybody on to the boat and set of. They could see that the Kayopo were thinking of throwing down spears but figured they saw it would be a futile gesture as they were a good bit away.

Tam put a bandage they recovered from Charles's plane around Looma's ankle for a bit of support. She winced most of the time and it worried Tam that her ankle might after all, be broken.

For the next few hours, the waters were calm, as the river had widened out. Time was moving on and Davie was looking for somewhere to settle for the night. As the water was slow moving and quite shallow, Davie figured about five feet deep, they decided to "drop anchor", (or rather, the large stone) around 20 feet from the shore.

They ate some dried meat and sweet potato before settling for the night. It got cooler as the night went on, so they pulled the animal skins, they had with them over themselves to keep warm.

The Spirit of St. Andrew

For once, Davie envied Tam having Looma to curl up with as they lay under the canopied part at the front of the craft.

Davie stared up at the starry sky and wondered if it was the same stars they would be seeing back in Aberdeenshire. He thought about his early life on Drystanes Farm beside Dyce just outside Aberdeen itself. From there he remembered often seeing the aurora borealis when he and Jean stood outside the house on crisp clear winter nights. How he longed for those happy days.

The boat swayed gently from side to side, which Davie found soothing, and soon fell asleep with his happy thoughts intact.

As soon as daylight broke, they lifted the stone anchor and were off again. They continued with a nice easy flow as the river stayed quite wide. On occasion they would see a couple of natives who were usually pointing in their direction. They would hear all the sounds of the jungle and often saw Pauls of smoke rising in the distance, no doubt Shabono campfires.

Several hours passed and Davie noticed a narrowing of the river begin to develop. This was usually accompanied by a rise in the flow speed. The lads didn't mind this too much as it meant they were making further ground faster.

What did concern them though was the increase in noise as they went forward. It didn't take a genius to work out that there were rapids up ahead. They could see the ground stayed quite level further on, so it was most likely not a waterfall.

If these rapids are particularly vicious and they had had a lighter boat, say a dingy. They may have gotten out of the water and went down the side till the rapids subsided.

Sadly, that was out of the question with the craft that they had, not to mention the fact that Looma could barely walk. No, the lads knew that any rough waters they came on they just had to, "go for it". They also knew that doing that increased the chances of damage to the boat. Crashing of rocks, filling with water, capsizing, were just some of the posable dangers. What they feared most were the inflatables being pierced and losing their buoyancy.

With little warning they were into white water, which caused Looma to scream virtually none stop. Like some youth on a roller coaster at a large fairground she screamed incessantly.

Though Davie wanted to, he didn't have time to tell her to "shut the fuck up", as his mind was solely on guiding the "Spirit of St Andrew" through these rapids. Water was in Davie and Tam's faces all the time as the boat soared up and then down through the narrow gully they had found themselves in. It was quite exhausting trying to get the rudder to keep the boat in a straight line. Tam was trying his best with the oars but was afraid of breaking them on the rocks which were about four feet away on either side.

After about half an hour of incessant white water the river began to widen out again and it seemed as if they had managed to avert tragedy, for now at least.

Davie and Tam slumped down on to the floor of the boat as Looma at last stopped her screaming. They then drew the boat into the side to assess any damage which may have occurred and to bail out the water which had built up in the bottom of the boat.

They were lucky enough to find a sandy beach about ten feet long, probably the sand built up from being washed down the rapids over many years. It was now nice and sunny, so they decided to bide a while to let things dry out including their clothes and bedding.

While they were stopped, they ate some food but were always vigilant as to local natives and wild animals. Davie remembered what Charles said about the Huaorani Indians and how vicious they were. He figured that the distance they had come put them right into Huaorani territory.

They were soon on their way again and glad of the widening of the river once more. It wasn't long before it started to rain, and rain it did. Hard rain straight down. They had strewn their bedding across the boat to stop it from filling up with water although it still got in through the sides.

Time was getting on and Davie knew if the rain stayed on, it may be futile to drop anchor mid-stream for the night as it could quickly fill up with rainwater. They needed somewhere on land to stop for the night.

The river was at its widest they had seen so far and up ahead Davie spotted an island in the river. The river was branching off to both sides of a small piece of land that had bits of forest and vegetation within it.

"Let's pull in there Tam, maybe even get a fire going to dry things out and get a bit of heat into us." Shouted Davie.

"Good idea mate....." said Tam, "......thank God the rains stopped. I see Looma's starting to get the shivers."

They pulled on to the stony beach area and secured the boat. Tam went into the small, wooded area, and gathered light firewood and soon they had a fire going, grateful to the Yanomami for showing them just how firelighting was done using the rope for friction on a dry piece of wood.

"It's good to get a heat Tam, but I'm wonderin' if it's wise to have a fire. I mean there's bound to be plenty natives about here."

"Naw, we'll be fine. We're on an island here Davie, we're twenty yards fae the shore in front o' us, and there's another twenty yards o' water from the other side o' this island to the other shore.... we'll be fine."

Knowing they were on an island did erase some of the fears Davie had, and soon he was off to sleep.

Looma rose to relieve herself and when she returned from the shrubbery, she was shaking Tam ferociously.

"Huaorani……Hourani!" She said in a loud whisper causing Tam and Davie to jump from their sleep.

As they rose and looked toward the shrubbery of the island, sure enough there they were five Huaorani warriors armed with spears and blowpipes. With spears raised they slowly approached the three travellers.

"Bastards must have come from the other side in canoes. What the fuck do we do Tam?" Demanded Davie.

"Get into the boat and get tae fuck oot o' here." Was Tam's response.

Tam took Loomas arm and slowly they all backed towards the boat. The Huaorani were mumbling amongst themselves, and they looked ready to charge.

The boat was still around 15 feet away from Tam, Looma and Davie, and the lads had figured the Huaorani were up for a fight.

"Right! Let's go!" Shouted Davie, as the three turned to run for the boat.

A spear whizzed past Tam's ear as the natives started their charge. It was then that disaster struck when Looma's ankle gave out and she fell in a heap just behind Tam.

"Tam!" She yelled just as one of the natives grabbed her by the arm. Tam was ready for it as he turned back and pulled Charles pistol from his pocket. He didn't hesitate and fired a round off into the air. The sheer volume of the sound caused the natives to run back a few yards before turning again.

Tam stood waving the pistol around to try and stir more fear into the Huaorani. Looma was trying to get to her feet. She was just out of reach of Tam who was gesturing to her to come to him. That was when another of the natives grabbed her by the arm once more.

Tam immediately pointed the gun at the native and pulled the trigger only for the gun to make a clicking noise…….. it was empty.

"Tam for fuck's sake come on!" Shouted Davie who was by now at the boat and was pushing it into the water.

Tam was trapped in a dilemma as he pondered whether to try and wrestle Looma away from her captor or give up and save his own skin.

Looma was calling to him, and Davie was yelling at him, as another spear grazed his shoulder, and a dart flew past him.

"Fuck…Fuck!" He roared, as he turned and made for the sensible option of the boat.

Davie was aware of a spear as well as darts whizzing past him as he pushed the boat of with Tam aboard, all the time cursing the Huaorani as he started to row.

He looked back only to see Looma pleading for him to come back while trying to wrestle free from her captors. The Huaorani were dancing around as if celebrating a great victory having captured a young native woman.

Davie was watching Tam row and cuss at the same time as he steered the boat away from the danger. As he did, he was shocked to see a dart hanging from Tams upper arm.

"Tam....Tam!" He shouted louder to get his attention.

"What!" Roared Tam in great anger.

"Your arm mate........there's a dart sticking in it." Said Davie in a calmer voice.

"What the........" went Tam as he swept the dart away with his hand, "Jesus Davie, do you think it was poisoned?"

"D'know Tam, time will tell.........." Said Davie apprehensively, "......but it didnae seem tae be right intae ye, which had to be good."

"Aye....good.... well, here's hopin'."

Davie was watching Tam all the time as they cruised quietly down with the flow, looking for any kind of reaction from his encounter with the dart.

Davie was looking around the boat and realised they had taken off without the animal skins they used for cover at night. Fortunately, the remaining food was there. He was annoyed at being snuck up on by the Huaorani. Annoyed that he never gave thought to them coming from the far side of the island. Annoyed that he allowed himself to light the fire which was obviously the attraction for the Huaorani to investigate.

A few more hours downstream and Davie was starting to feel concern for Tam who was showing signs of drowsiness. He knew Tam was never one to sleep during the daytime and it worried him.

As it was, there were now more things to worry the big man. The river was narrowing once again and, in the distance, he could hear what he now recognised as roaring rapid waters.

"Tam!" he shouted, causing Tam to jump, a little startled.

"What......what?" He mumbled as he came to himself.

"Rapids......dead ahead......." was Davies terse, loud, reply, ".... Beter brace yersel' big man."

"Jesus!" Exclaimed a shocked Davie, as he looked down stream at the channel of profuse white foam tossing wildly in all directions. He could see how narrow the passageway was to become further down, and he realised they were in for one hell of a ride.

Steering became pointless, the craft was being thrown in all directions. Davie grabbed one of the oars from Tam as the two men did their utmost to keep the boat afloat and away from the rocks on either side. Frighteningly the "Spirit of St Andrew" suddenly rose about five feet in the air before crashing back down into the violently turbulent waters, at that point the risen nose of the craft broke away with a loud cracking noise.

"We've lost the top off the bow Davie!" Roared Tam, as down the river they sped, trying to control the boat, but knowing it was nye well impossible.

"Fuck me!" Shouted Davie as the boat suddenly plunged downwards nose first over a fall of around 10 feet. When they hit the bottom, the boat was then shot up into the air once more, only this time it turned 180 degrees in the air sending everyone and everything flying out of the boat.

Down they went into the foaming waters. Davie didn't know which way was up as he struggled to find equilibrium. Eventually he broke surface and gulped in air. He looked around desperately for his friend but could only see white foam. He then felt himself go over another fall. Only this time it threw him into calmer waters. He had reached the end of the rapids.

Davie waded over to the shore and flopped down on to a large, rounded rock. He turned just in time to see the remains of the "Spirit of St Andrew" sink out of sight and watched the oars float off downstream.

More concerning was the whereabouts of Tam as he was nowhere to be seen. Davie started to call out for his friend, as he did, he walked of in a downstream direction, calling out as he went.

Then, on the other side of the river about 100 yards from where the water softened out, Davie saw what looked like a bundle of clothing lying over a large stone. He took off, splashing threw the knee-deep waters till he arrived at what was indeed his friend.

Tam was face down before Davie turned him over, "Tam....Tam.... are you ok?"

To Davies relief, Tam coughed and spluttered before saying, "Never better."

The two then sat together, their backs against the big rock Tam had been on.

Davie was trying to gather himself and was trying to figure out just what the hell they could do from here on in. They were on a riverbank in the middle of the rainforest with no craft to sail in. They had no food, no cover, were open to the elements not to mention the wildlife and natives, and on top of all that it did look like Tam was suffering from the effects of dart frog poisoning.

Davie sat recalling what Charlie said the Yanomami told him about the poison.

Yes, it could kill a monkey as well as other small animals. Humans it could kill as well but more than likely a full-grown man is more likely to become ill for quite a period of time.

The thought of what Charlie said gave Davie hope that a big man like Tam, who, in fact didn't have the dart right into him, should in fact be alright after a while.

The Spirit of St. Andrew

Davie reckoned it was about mid-day as he looked all around him. All he could see was dense forest all around with a river running through it. Just ahead the river took a turn in what he knew was an easterly direction. He knew they were now set to be travelling on foot and that that was the direction they needed to go in by continuing to follow the river.

"So, Tam are you up for a walk?" He asked his friend jovially.

"Walk..." said Tam, "......I don't know if I can stand mate."

Davie helped Tam to his feet where he said he was feeling fine. As they spoke something caught Davies eye about 200 yards up stream on the riverbank near the end of the rapids, it was four Indian natives, and one of them was pointing towards the two of them. He wasn't sure if they were Huaorani following up on the earlier encounter, but he wasn't about to hang around and find out.

"Fuck!" Shouted Davie.

"What....what is Mate?" Asked Tam.

"Natives.......and they've spotted us.... come on, let's get tae fuck oot o' here."

The two of them started off as quickly as they could downstream but it was heavy going as Tam kept stumbling about. Davie glanced around and was horrified to see that the natives had set off after them at a fair pace.

He considered going into the water and swimming with the flow downstream, but worried about Tam's ability to make such an effort.

They went around the bend Davie had seen earlier, and he figured it would be only a couple of minutes before the natives were upon them. He was gutted at the thought of having come this far and being captured once again by rainforest Indians.

"Davie..." said Tam, ".... what's that up ahead at the side o' the river?"

Davie looked up and couldn't believe what he saw. The two inflatables, lodged between two rocks and they were still inflated.

"Yes Tam, there is a God after all......" Shouted Davie, ".......come on let's get this rigged up and away."

Davie was pleased to see all the cord attached to the inflatable was still there, and even more pleased to see the two wooden oars tangled in with the rope.

Quickly, he decided to join the two sections together rather than one behind the other. He did this with the cord and fix an oar underneath for them to place their feet on as they moved through the water. This would leave him the other oar to help steer their new craft down the river.

He got Tam astride one inflatable and himself alongside him on the other, before he pushed off into the river with the other oar. They were only a matter of thirty seconds away when the natives ran into view. Tam couldn't resist waving a couple of fingers at the bewildered Indians.

Davie was happy with their setup on the makeshift craft. With one of them at either side they were well balanced and relatively comfortable.

"Where we Goin' Davie?" Asked a groggy Tam.

"Haven't a fuckin' clue mate......" Was Davies terse reply, ".... but we'll get there!"

They floated for quite a time, the pace of the river being relatively easy, was making steering comfortable. Tam had his head down on the inflatable and was asleep. This caused Davie to keep alert as it would not take much for Tam to roll over into the water and he knew he would have quite a job retrieving him, never mind getting him back on to the makeshift boat.

Davie himself had a strong desire to sleep as well. How easy would it be to just lay his head down as Tam was going and drop off. Thing is, it was the thought of the "dropping off," that kept Davie focused.

Davie was aware the day was creeping on, late afternoon he reckoned. He was in the arms of a dilemma whether to make for the shore for the night, or, to keep going and hope for the best.

The Spirit of St. Andrew

As his mind raced, he became suddenly aware of a change in sound coming from up ahead. "Jesus......" he thought, "......not more rapids, please."

He soon realised the sound was somewhat different from what he had heard before, more of a whooshing sound than a rumble.

It was then he saw that the river he was on was suddenly widening right out, right out into something huge, it was the Amazon River.

Suddenly the waters became more turbulent, though not destructive. It reminded him of being in the water at Aberdeen beach on a tractor tyre tube. Great fun as the thing bobbed up and down as the tide came in, throwing spray into your face. This motion woke Tam who immediately grabbed the cords around the dingy and held on for dear life. It was as if the Amazon was annoyed at this little river pushing in from the side, how dare it have the tenacity to barge into such a great waterway.

It soon settled once the great river had swallowed up the small estuary.

Davie looked around and saw that they were well away from any shore and up ahead the chasm only got wider and wider.

"Jesus...." Said Davie, "......we're heading for the Atlantic Ocean."

"...Take us a wee while to cross that than Davie." Said Tam drowsily.

Davie smiled, "That's the way Tam, keep that sense of humour going."

Davie look to the far shores as light faded and saw fires starting to glow. Were they the fires of native Indians, or fires of civilisation? If he could be certain, it was the later, he might make a real effort at steering their craft towards it, far though it was.

He then decided in his mind to take stock of their situation and it didn't make for good reading.

He thought, "Both of us exhausted, hungry, thirsty, with Tam a little worse. There was now no doubt that Tam had been poisoned by the dart. Even if we wanted to, we didn't have the strength to make a Bringe for the far shore where the lights are. So, what do we do?"

CHAPTER 19.
INTO THE OCEAN.

Although they were still under the influence of the Amazon River, Davie and Tam were now in the Atlantic Ocean. The brown silty waters of the river were visible to Davie. He in fact, had heard that the waters of the Amazon are still prevalent 12 miles out to sea, such is the power of the Amazon.

It was still dark and the desire for Davie to put his head down on to the inflatable and sleep was almost overpowering. Because Tam was asleep beside him, he knew it would be crazy for him to nod off. Somebody had to make sure they remained on the makeshift craft.

Davies head was rolling around as his eyes flickered, fighting to stay open. Davie nodded off. In his dazed state he thought he heard something splash. He worried of course about sharks and woke with a start, only to realise that Tam was not beside him.

"Fuck......!" He shouted, "......Tam......!" then again, ".... Tam, where the fuck are you, you big bastard!"

The waters were dead calm and there was no sight of Tam anywhere. Instinctively, Davie rolled over into the waters and dived down looking around frantically for his friend. Suddenly he saw a hazy shape about 15 feet away from him. Davie swam frantically towards this shape and sure enough it was Tam. He didn't seem conscious to Davie and although the water restricted him, Davie slapped Tam on the face as hard as he could causing him to jar awake.

The two swam as hard as they could to the surface, both gulping a huge breath when they broke surface, whereupon Tam coughed and spluttered as he cleared the sea water from his lungs.

The next problem for Davie was getting Tam back on to the inflatable, he had expired whatever energy he had swimming to the surface. He told Tam to grab the cords of the craft as he lifted his leg on to the boat as he did Davie's side of the craft rose up causing the two of them to fall back into the water. Davie then instructed Tam to hold on while he made his way to the other inflatable, Davie pulled himself aloft before grabbing hold of Tam and rugging him on.

Now that he was on, Davie then tied Tam's shirt tail to one of the cords of the boat, at least if he fell off again, it wouldn't be far.

"Davie......" Said Tam, "........are we going to die tonight?"

"Are we fuck, and don't you dare talk to me like that again." Was Davies desperate reply.

The Spirit of St. Andrew

Who knows how long had passed since the "falling in" but Davie was aware that they couldn't last much longer. Another coupe over the side and that would be the end of them, for neither had the strength to get back on to the inflatables.

Davies head was rolling once more as he tried to concentrate on the stars above. It was a beautiful clear night and he was amazed at the enormity of what he was looking at. He then started to wonder about his own mortality and if there was a superior being up there in that great cosmos looking down in him and Tam right now. Was he preparing to judge them. Davie fleeted through his life and wondered at his chances of being accepted by this great creator.

"My God...." He thought, ".....I killed a few men in the war, poor bastards, what about that kid I stuck with my bayonette, looked about 16. Still, I saved a few lives as well in the trenches......."

Unaware of it, Davie was falling asleep as he started to roll to the side. Almost instinctively he knew he was going in.

Suddenly, and inexplicably, something seemed to push Davie back on to the craft.

"What the fuck....." He said, as he jerked up and then looked down.

To Davies amazement he saw the head of a dolphin, its eyes looking into his as if to say, "are you ok."

Davie knew that if he had gone into the water, it was the end. He knew he could never pull himself up again. He wanted to shake Tam conscious to tell him what had just happened, but he thought twice about telling his friend that a dolphin had just saved his life. Who the hell would believe what just happened he would be laughed at by everyone he told. He could hear them ridicule him, "Aye right, a bloody dolphin pushed ye up on tae the boat, what did it do next, tuck ye in!"

Davie looked all around to see if he could see the beast again, but it was nowhere to be seen. He wondered if he had just experienced a full-blown miracle, for the last thing on his mind was about there being or not being a God. Had God read Davie's thoughts and then delivered him from the jaws of death.

As he looked around, he suddenly noticed a light in the near distance, and it seemed to be coming towards them.

"Tam....Tam, wake up, I think it's a boat."

"Yer delusional Davie, can ye no see that we are fucked mate!"

"Am tellin' ye, it's a fuckin' boat and it's comin' this way."

Davie now saw the outline of the ship though still a bit away. Davie also knew how much distance it took for a ship to stop and that there was a strong possibility that it could steam right past them without a soul on board seeing them.

That was when he remembered the flare gun that Charlie had given him. His hand felt to the side where he holstered the gun and to his horror couldn't feel it.

"No.....no....." He called out, before searching further round his midriff. Suddenly he felt the gun, it had ridden around his waist, probably when he was recovering Tam from the water.

He took the gun out and cocked the firing pin, then hesitated.

"Wait a minute....." He thought, "........I've got just one shot to get it right here. If I fire too soon, they may not see the damned thing.......at the same time if I fire too late the ship could roll right past us!"

Keeping all of that in mind he decided to fire when he figured the ship was around a mile away, that way they would be near enough to see the flare and yet be far enough away to give the vessel time to at least slow down.

Next thing to perplex Davie was the question as to whether the damned flare gun would indeed fire. After all Charlie must have had it for at least three years without using the damned thing.

The time soon came when the ship was at, what Davie reckoned was the right distance away, so he held the gun in the air and pulled the trigger.

Boom! Of it went, shooting up at least one hundred yards and glowing bright red. And o' what joy when only around a minute after, a couple of search lights went on aboard the front of the ship and started scanning the waters.

The ship had slowed right down when it arrived at the dingy. Men on board were ready with a long rope which they threw down to Davie and Tam. Davie grabbed the rope and fixed it to the inflatable.

As he finished tying the rope, he looked up at the ship which he figured to be around the same size as the "Empress of Glasgow". Then he stared at the name on the ships side, "Santa Margaretta", which he assumed was the "Saint Margaret", fine, he thought, probably Spanish. Then, to his horror he saw the writing under the name in big letters, "SAVANTA".

"Jesus......" Thought Davie, ".......... of all the ships in the Atlantic Ocean, and there must be thousands, they had to be picked up by one from Savanta the City where they had not long ago been condemned to die."

CHAPTER 20.
OUT OF THE FRYING PAN........

The ship's crew eyed the lads with curiosity as they escorted them to the captain's quarters. Tam had to be helped by a couple of the men although they both showed signs of fatigue.

The captain, a dark-haired short man, not more than 5'6", stood and stared at the lads for a while. Davie was about to ask if he spoke English and soon got his answer.

Like Charles had done the captain ran through the different languages from Portuguese to Spanish, then Frensh, before alighting on English.

"Yes, English......well, Scottish actually." Said Davie.

"Scottish......." repeated the captain, "......Well, Scottish, my name is Captain Brown, as it turns out my father was English, my mother Beldovian."

He then paced from side to side with his arms behind his back, this causing his potbelly to protrude even more that it had. He then stopped and turned to the lads.

The Spirit of St. Andrew

"How in the name of God did you come to be in the Atlantic Ocean on a....a..... makeshift craft?" He asked.

Tam raised his head, and answered sarcastically, "We were sunbathing on the shore and got swept out to sea...... bloody ebb tide."

"Agh...the British sense of humour......very funny.....em....mister...?" he gestured to Tam for his name.

"Goodison.....Tomas Goodison."

"And you sir?" He asked Davie.

"David Harley." Answered Davie.

"Tomas Goodison and David Harley...now......correct me if I'm wrong gentlemen but aren't you the two men who were convicted of murder in our lovely city?" He quizzed sarcastically.

"Wrongly convicted Sir, we were set up." Said Davie.

"That aside gentlemen, just how in the name of God did you get away from the "Hellhole"?"

Davie then felt he had to intervene and change the subject, "Captain Brown, you seem like a fair man to me and I'm sure we'll fill you in on all of that, but we haven't eaten in days nor slept properly either. My friend here is ill after being poisoned by a native Indian dart and needs medication."

The captain took a minute to think before answering, "Of course, after all, we're not barbarians......" he nodded to one of his men beside the lads and told them in Spanish to the effect, "......take then down and give them food and somewhere to rest up.... but keep them under surveillance......and have the ships medical officer look at the sick one."

Davie and Tam didn't know how long they had slept but Davie felt much the better for it. Tam still had a haziness about him but was sitting up, as one of the crew came to bring them to the captain.

"Ah gentlemen, did you sleep well?" Said the captain on their arrival.

Davie and Tam nodded.

"Good..." He continued, "......Gentlemen, as you probably know by now, you are aboard the good ship "Saint Margaret" "bound for Boston in the United States. We left Savanta two week ago where we went to Beuna's Aries in Argentina. We took on beef and wine there for delivery to the USA. I really should turn back to Savanta and delivery you to the authorities there. After all it's only a full day's journey back. The problem is we were held up in Argentina and are already running late so you gentlemen will have to be held in custody till we are back in Savanta."

Davie listened to the captain closely before speaking, "Captain Brown, if you are familiar with our story, you will know that we ourselves are merchant seamen......"

"Yes, I am aware of that."

"The thing is, rather than being cooped up in some cabin, we......or at least I, would be prepared to work our...... my, passage. I mean there's bound to be something you can find for us to do?"

"A noble gesture sir, which I will probably take you up on, after all it will be a good four days before we alight on Boston. By the way, out medical officer said Mr Goodison is very lucky to be alive and will perhaps take quite some time to fully recover if in fact he does."

Tam looked up from his malaise, "Tell your medical officer, thank you for his diagnosis and that I have every intention of making a full recovery."

"Ah, the Scottish grit......I like that." Said Captain Brown with a large grin.

The lads were taken back to their cabin, it was small, with two beds, one atop the other. The door was always lock after they were put in. A bucket was installed for personal use as well as a large tin jug full of water. There was also a magazine on the small table for them to read.

"Welcome to the Ritz........" Said Davie, as he picked up the magazine, "........and a magazine, in Spanish!"

"The shitz, mare like......." Replied Tam before going on, "........Listen Davie. I've made up my mind that if they start takin' us back to Savanta efter Boston, I'm goin' tae find a way of throwin' masel overboard afore we get there."

"Is that you givin' up on me again Goodison. Listen, there's a hell of a lot o' water tae pass under the bridge afore we head back to bloody Savanta, and don't you forget it. No no, Tam, it's Boston here we come."

"Boston......." Said Tam with a twist in his face, "......haven't you got a brother there?"

"That I do Tomas...." Replied Davie as he hoisted himself on to the upper bunk, "......and I'm going to try my darndest at getting a message to him."

"Brilliant, Davie, that would be brilliant."

Two days later the sun was shining brightly on the "Santa Margaretta" as it cruised northward through the Atlantic Ocean. As he expected, Davie was issued with paint brush and a pot of white paint and ordered to paint the ships rails. He watched as the crew went about their business, scrubbing the decks and helping with the painting.

As he watched Davie was attention was drawn to one of the men.

"Jesus, I know that bastard!" He thought to himself, then again, "No...it canny be."

Davie took another hard look at the man, "Jesus, it is him, the fuckin' peasant that was in the casino and testified against us.........that's right, in court they said one o' them was a merchant seaman......the little bastard."

He was a good bit away from Davie who decided to bide his time and wait till he was a lot closer to him before

The Spirit of St. Andrew

pinning him down. Meantime Davie was trying to remember the man's name, but it just would not come to him.

Another day passed and once more Davie was painting on deck. He had told Tam about the man and Tam told him to get hold of the "wee shite" and confront him about that night.

Davie saw his chance as the Savanta peasant came walking towards him. Davie stepped right out in front of him, causing him to freeze on the spot with a look of terror in his eyes.

"Agh....." said Davie, "......so you do know me then?"

The peasant knew he was cornered, "Si signor, when I heard that two prisoners from the "Hellhole" had been picked up, I knew it would be you."

"Your English is good." Said Davie.

"Yes, I've sailed with captain Brown for two years now and he teach me."

"So....." said Davie, getting straight to the point, ".......why the hell did you and your friend lie about us in court?"

He seemed keen to talk, "You don't understand signor, we were threatened not just by the Police but by the family of Jose Ramires........"

"The man that was stabbed to death?" Interrupted Davie.

"Si signor."

"So…….wait a minute, what's your name?" Asked Davie.

"Diago……..Diago Fernandes."

"Ok Diago, who the hell actually stabbed Mr Ramires?"

Diago then pulled away, "I'm sorry signor, but I must return to work."

Davie called after him as he sped away, "Don't worry Diago, I'll be talking to you later."

That evening, Davie spoke to Tam about what had just happened.

"Right," Said Tam, "We go to the captain and tell him about this wee conniving' bastard."

"Good idea Tam……. "Said Davie, "……but I've an idea this "wee connivin' bastard" will just deny everything. He'll probably say we're desperate and are tryin' tae blame whoever the hell we can."

"So……" continued Tam, "…….what the hell do we do Davie?"

"Don't know mate, but we better do it before this ship leaves Boston."

CHAPTER 21.
A HELPING HAND.

When Helen Harley answered her door in Froghall Gardens in Aberdeen, she was surprised to see William Smythe standing there.

Well, well, Mr Smythe isn't it, nice to see you again, do come in."

Smythe went in and sat opposite Helen once again. After the niceties Smythe got to the point.

"The reason I'm here Miss Harley......"

"Please, William, it's Helen."

"Of course, Helen....the reason I'm here is to depart some good news."

"Brilliant!" Said Helen, nodding at Smythe to continue.

"The thing is your father is most definitely alive."

"O' thank God......" Said Helen as her hand went to her mouth as she almost burst into tears ".... where is he?"

The Spirit of St. Andrew

"Right Helen, here's the downside if you like. He's on board a ship heading to Boston. They were picked up in the ocean by a ship out of…… well of all place Savanta."

"Savanta," Said Helen, slightly concerned now, "But isn't that the city they were imprisoned in?"

"Yes, we found out all this because the captain of the ship telegrammed back to Savanta to say they had picked them up and was to return them after they had been to Boston. I still have friends in Savanta who find out about all these things and telegrammed me."

"So, is there anything we can do to stop them returning to Savanta?" Asked Helen.

"The thing is Helen I came here to ask if you thought Davies brother would have any clout in Boston, or could muster anyone to help get them of the ship?"

"Uncle Wull is quite the businessman out there. Let's get in touch William".

CHAPTER 22.
BOSTON.

The "Saint Margaret" was fortunate enough to get a mooring on the quay side of Boston harbour. This was good news for the lads as they knew they could just as easily be anchored in the harbour a few days waiting for a berth.

On the approach to the harbour, while Davie was painting outside, he decided to corner Diago once more. It wasn't long before he walked past, and Davie took his chance.

"Listen Diago we know that you know me, and my friend, are innocent of killing Jose Ramirez."

"Si." Said Diago hesitantly.

"Ok then, how would you like to help us sort this out."

Diago shrugged his shoulders, "But what can I do Signor?"

"Tell me Diago, are you due shore leave here in Boston?" Quizzed Davie sternly.

The Spirit of St. Andrew

"Si."

"Good, then I want you to deliver a message for me to someone I know...will you do that?" Asked Davie almost pleadingly.

"Alright Signor, but I don't go ashore till the evening."

"That's ok...." Said Davie, "......come to my cabin before you go and bring a pencil and paper.......can you do that?" He pleaded once more.

"Si...I'll do that."

Sure enough, that evening Diago unlocked their cabin door and entered, looking around for other men as he did. He handed Davie the pencil and paper, whereupon Davie proceeded to write.

"Being held on board Savanta ship the "Sata Margaretta" docked on the quayside. Need immediate help. Your brother Davie".

Davie, having visited Wull before, knew the address, and wrote it on the other side of the piece of paper and gave it to Diago.

"It's only a couple of streets up from the harbour. Good luck." Said Davie as Diago left, locking their cabin door after him.

"I dinny trust that wee shite Davie." Said Tam, who had come round only minutes earlier.

"Well Tam, right now, he's all we've got."

A few hours passed and once more Tam was out like a light. Davie was pacing about in the cabins small area wondering when in the hell Diago would return and whether he had got the message to his brother.

Davie stopped pacing when he heard the cabin key turn in the lock. He looked on wide eyed as the door opened, hoping beyond hope that it would be Wull come to rescue them from their hell on earth.

Davie got a double shock when he saw it was Diago and that he was pointing a pistol in his direction.

"What the fuck is this?" Quizzed Davie.

"You, signor, must come with me with your hands raised please." Said Diago, as he waved the pistol to indicate to Davie to move out of the cabin.

"What's all this about Diago, where the hell are you taking me?"

"Not far signor Harley....soon it will be all over." Said Diago as he locked the cabin once they were out.

"Well...." Said Davie, "......I take it you didn't get to my brother?"

Diago then removed the note that Davie had written from his pocket and crumpled it up in front of Davie.

"That'll be a "no" then."

The Spirit of St. Andrew

"I'm sorry signor, but I can't have you go free and put the blame on me. Nor can I have you going back to Savanta and blaming me there either."

"So, you're going to shoot me?"

"Si signor.... I have no choice. I will say you got out of your cabin, and you went to attack me, and I had to shoot." He said with a shrug of the shoulders.

"Ok......" Said Davie, "......but before you shoot me can you tell me exactly what happened that night outside the casino?"

"Sure..." Diago said, ".... after you left my brother and I were ordered to assist Jose Ramires out the back along with the big guy who was dealing. Yes?"

"Yes, I saw you all go out."

"On the way out the big man, you know, he dealt the cards......" Davie nodded, "......he said he needed to relieve himself and went into a toilet at the back. We went out with Ramirez and he was shouting and cursing us for not stopping you from hitting him......he went crazy with the anger and took a swipe at my brother. That was when my brother drew a knife and stabbed Ramirez. He then pulled the knife out and gave it to me, so I stabbed him again. By this time, he was dead."

"So, you and your brother killed Jose Ramirez."

"Si. When the big man, you know, the dealer, came out he demanded to know what happened. That was when my brother said that you and your friend were waiting outside and stabbed him. You see we saw your friend remove the knife from the table in the casino, so we knew you had a knife."

The two arrived at the foot of the stair leading up to the deck area.

"You're forgetting one thing Diago." Said Davie.

"...and what would that be signor?"

"My friend Tam, he'll still deny all the accusations and say he saw you remove me from the cabin."

"Signor, I saw the state your friend was in just now, barely conscious....it will be easy to put a pillow over his face and say he had passed away due to the poison." Said Diago, with a sarcastic smile.

"So, you've got it all figured out." Said Davie.

"Si, now I want you to kneel down on the step. This will be quick, and you should feel nothing. Now, turn away." Said Diago, as he held his arm out straight in readiness to fire.

Davie seemed to have no option as he turned around, his hands still in the air. It was then he braced himself for the sound of the gun and for all to go dark.

BANG! Went the gun. Davie grimaced. Then, nothing, nothing but the sound of two men grappling. He turned quickly only to see Tam behind Diago with his arm around his neck and his other hand holding Diago's armed hand in the air.

Davie was on him like a shot and took the gun from him as Tam threw Diago to the ground.

"You, ok?" Said Tam, breathing heavily.

"Sure...." said Davie, "......but how in the hell did you get out of the cabin, I saw Diago lock it as we left."

"Old trick I saw in the pictures in a film, I saw a chap put a newspaper under a door and knock the key out of the keyhole and onto the paper which he pulled back under the door." Said Tam shrugging his shoulders.

"Right..." Said Davie, "......the Spanish magazine."

"Thats it Davie. Had to break up your wooden spoon to get the key pushed out though."

"My wooden spoon, why the hell didn't you break yours."

"Very funny.......so, what do we do now Mr Harley."

"We get to fuck of this damned boat.... that's what."

"The captain will shoot you if you try to leave." Said Diago.

"Will he now......" Snapped Tam, as he grabbed Diago and pushed him on in front of them, "......then there will be a damned good chance he'll shoot you as well ye murdering wee bastard.......get on!"

The Spirit of St. Andrew

Captain Brown and his men had been aroused by the gun shot and were all on deck as Tam and Davie surfaced with Diago in front of them, the gun pointed at his head. Davie noticed the captain had a pistol as did two of his men.

"Captain Brown...." Davie shouted, "........this man has confessed to us that it was he and his brother who killed Jose Ramirez in Savanta and not us. Now, all we want to do is leave your ship peaceably and with no fuss.... what do you say?"

Suddenly Diago shouted out, "Do not listen to them captain, it was they who killed Ramirez."

Davie and Tam could feel the tension mounting and a stand-off seemed imminent. One thing Davie was certain of was that they were leaving this boat come hell or high water.

It was then that everyone became aware of some men boarding the ship via the gangway. There were three armed men behind a fourth, who was holding some papers in his hand.

"The captain spoke towards them, "Who are you men and what are you doing on my ship?"

The man with the papers spoke, "Captain I have here a letter signed by J Edger Hoover himself, demanding that you release two men you are holding, namely David Harley and Tomas Goodison with immediate effect. These men are from a country allied to the United States and we believe they were falsely incarcerated in your country. Furthermore, if you do not release these men your ship will never be able to do trade with the United States ever again......do you understand all of this captain?"

The papers were handed to the captain who looked at them before speaking, "Well gentlemen it would seem you have arrived at a very appropriate moment, for our "prisoners" as you referred to them have just, it seems, been put in a position to prove their innocence........"

On hearing these words, a furious looking Diago broke free from Davie and grabbed a gun from one of the captain's men and made to aim it at Davie. For the second time that night Davie waited for a bullet to enter his body as once more a loud bang went off. Once again, he was unscathed as he then saw the shot was fired by captain Brown straight at Diago who collapsed into a heap on deck.

As soon as he fired the captain then ordered his men to stand down as guns were being raised everywhere. Pretty soon calm was restored. When that happened Davie, to most people's surprise, went over and embraced the man who had read from the papers, it was of course his brother Wull.

"How in hell did you know about us Wull, I tried to get a message to you, but the little bastard just told us he never delivered it?" He demanded.

"You brother, have a very resourceful daughter. She and a chap named William Smythe, telegrammed me about your predicament and.......here I am."

Soon, Davie and Tam were in Wull's "fancy car", as Tam called it, heading for his home.

"Wull, how long have you known J Edger Hoover?" Asked Davie.

"I've never met the man......" Said Wull, "......it was a huge bluff, but it was all we could come up with in the time we had, the thing is......it's worked."

When they got back to Wull's house Davie was glad to see all his family once more. It wasn't long before Tam was asleep on Wull's sofa.

"What the hell's wrong we Tam, Davie?" Asked Wull.

Davie explained what happened to Tam and all they'd been through.

When Wull left the room Davie took a moment to talk to Fiona.

"My God Fiona your looking as beautiful as ever. America must be good for you?"

Fiona gave a wry smile, "Thank you David....I wish I could say the same for you. You look like you've been dragged through a hedge backwards."

Davie smiled, "......Aye, it's been a rough few month......I could write a book."

"Then perhaps you should." She said as Wull returned.

"Listed Davie..." Said Wull, as he looked at Tam on the settee, ".... I know a doctor here who has some radical new medicine, discovered by a Scotsman no less, calls it penicillin, it might just help Tam."

"Sounds great Wull, but we've nae money for medical stuff........."

Wull cut in, "Shut up ye big gowk, I'll take care of it."

Three weeks passed and Davie was desperate to get home and was delighted when Wull informed him that there was a ship heading over and that he could work his passage if he was willing.

Davie jumped at the chance but was taken by surprise when Tam informed him that he would not be going with him.

"Look Davie, Wull's had me working in his cigarette factory as you know, and I kind of like it and the medicine he got me has worked wonders, so I think, if it's ok we Wull, that I'll stay."

And so, it turned out that two seemingly inseparable pals were indeed, for the first time in twenty years, to go their separate ways.

CHAPTER 23.
HOME AT LAST.

When Davie returned home to a loving welcome from his son and daughter, he decided to work on his family's farm for a while at least. Drystanes of Dyce, now run by his sister Cathy and her man Jack, the farm having been in the family for some time. Davie saw Cathy become more like their mother, she had her ways and mannerisms, though perhaps a little fistier than she. Cathy was in her early forties now and her two children who, like Davies son and daughter were in their late teens and worked in Aberdeen. Cathy's husband Jack, or "black Jack" as he was known in the village due to his thick black beard, was, despite his somewhat fearsome look, a quiet individual who kept himself to himself.

Davie had been working for seven months at Drystanes since his return and although he was enjoying the work, he was aware of Cathy's continual bickering about how hard it was becoming to make ends meet, due particularly to the aftermath of the depression in the late 20's early

30's. During that time, they made the decision to move from beef to dairy, and it was proving a struggle.

Davie continually took cuts to his pay to try and help, this though only making it difficult financially for himself. He often considered going back to sea but thought it would not be the same without his long-time friend Tomas Goodison who, to all intent and purposes, was very happy working away in America. Letters from Davies brother Wull would tell of how much Tam enjoyed the work and of course, chasing the women of Boston, especially now that he had fully recovered from his bad bout of poisoning caused by the native Indians dart which pierced his arm during their flight to freedom.

One mid-week dinnertime, Davie sat at the dining table to find there were a couple of letters for him. One of the letters had a letter within it. The extra letter had been forwarded by his daughter Mary and had an official look about it.

Davie was surprised to find it was from the local government office and when he read it, he received quite a shocking surprise.

"That letter seems tae hae put a smile on yer face Davie, what's it about?" Asked Cathy as she sat supping her soup.

"Well......" Said Davie, "......would you believe, the government of Beldovia, having heard of me and Tams harsh treatment in their country, want to compensate us with a financial payment of £5,000."

"Wow!" went Cathy, "and I should think so too. Is that each, or between you?"

"Each......" Replied Davie, a large smile forming across his face, before he continued, ".......wait a minute, oh aye, here's the catch. We must go to Savanta to receive it, seemingly, Phillippe Ramon wants the world to see what a benevolent leader he is and insists he presents the money to us in person."

"And how the hell are you going to get there Davie, ah mean it's halfway across the world?" Asked Cathy.

"It seems I've to contact the local government office to find out......oh, and by the way, it says I can take a friend for company."

Cathy looked at Davie for a second then asked, "Do you really want to go back to that place Davie, efter the way they treated ye?"

"That's a good question Cath, mind you, efter the way they treated us they surely owe us some kind o' recompense and £5000 is a tidy sum and would go a long way towards helpin' the farm........but I'll wait and see what they say at the government office."

The Spirit of St. Andrew

Meanwhile over in Boston Tam was receiving the same information. He was reading the news to Wull who asked if he was going to go.

"Tell you what Wull.......I'll go if you'll go we me, it says I can take a friend......what do you say?"

"Jesus Tam, I'd really have to think about that one. "Was Wulls terse reply.

The Spirit of St. Andrew

Chapter 24.
RUNNING FOR YOUR LIFE.

Darkness was slowly creeping in around the camp of the Huaorani Indians of the Amazon rainforest. Looma, now over seven months pregnant was readying herself to make a run for it. She knew perfectly well that once the Huaorani saw the fairness of her baby's skin, they would undoubtedly kill it and probable eat it as well.

Since her capture on the island, she had been given to one of the Huaorani men, a fat, elderly, vulgar individual, who was as much her reason for getting away as was the danger to her unborn child.

As she lay beside him supposedly for the night, Looma listen for the chatter of the last few men to stop as they sat around the dying embers of the campfire. One by one they drifted away to their sleeping places till finally it fell silent. Silent that was but for the snoring of the men within the communal hut where the majority slept.

Unlike the Shabono she had been used to with her own people the Yanomami, the Huaorani built huts which were elevated above ground to around three feet, this was to allow for the high waters when the nearby river flooded at the hight of the rainy season.

Looma new by the sound of her man's snoring he was well into a deep sleep, and she decided it was time to make her move. Looma knew she had to make her move at night. Sure, she could disappear into the forest during daylight hours, but as soon as they became aware of her absence a search party of around four men would be sent after her and would soon catch her.

However, traveling at night, although slightly more difficult, she knew that, if all went well and they didn't miss her until morning, then she knew she would have a good head start on the search party.

Slowly she slipped from her bed, she knew the first major problem would be lifting the flap that cover the entrance to the shack because the damned thing always creaked. She figured the solution to this was to lift it ever so slowly, and only enough for her to squeeze out of the shack. Without disturbing anyone, she was outside. She investigated the dark with the aid of a bright moon and could see no one. She then tiptoed to the edge of the forest where she got the shock of her life, for there, facing her, was one of the Huaorani men relieving himself. She had to think quickly, or it was all over. Instinctively she crouched down and made to be having a pee herself. The man stared at her for a few seconds, gave off a grunt, then headed back to the compound.

The Spirit of St. Andrew

Once she recovered from that shock she took off. Fortunately, there was a well-trodden track to the river used frequently by the villagers when going fishing or bathing. Looma knew only too well that the river was the route she had to take to get back to her own people. She also knew she had a way to go, for she remembered travelling down the river with Davie and her man Tam and that they had stopped for two nights on that journey before she was captured on the island. All be it the end of the second night was the morning she was captured.

When she arrived at the river, she understood she was on the wrong side for finding her people and would have to cross at some point. She also remembered that the rivers depth and width altered frequently as it ebbed and flowed.

The moon remained clear that night and this helped Looma on her journey. Most of the way she was able to travel over the stony ground on the riverside, although on a couple of occasions she had to duck into the rainforest as the waters rose that bit higher and there was a lack of stones at the edge.

The young woman pressed on and soon saw up ahead, as daylight started to creep in, the rapids which caused her to scream with all her might on the way down. She was also aware that this was where the river narrowed in places and as she climbed over so many large rocks, she just could not find an area narrow enough to leap across. The rushing water gave off quite a crescendo of noise as she stood tall on one large stone looking back way down river to see if there was any sign of the Huaorani pursuing her. She peered strenuously but saw no one. She'd come a fair distance since she set out but knew she would not be stopping until the evening darkness set in.

She was aware she still had a way to go before her next milestone that she remembered on the way down. The waterfall.

Onward she plodded as the light once more started to fade. She was very conscious that on this night she needed to rest and started to look for safe place to lay up. While looking into the dense forest she noticed a large fallen tree which still bore its leaves. She then crawled into an area beneath the fallen tree that almost felt like she was crawling into a cave. After making sure there were no wild animals nor snakes within the covering, Looma snuggled in with her back against the large tree and pulled the dried leaves that were all around into herself and around her body, she felt quite snug as she relaxed feeling the movement of her unborn, and was soon off to sleep.

Davie was excited as he sat down with Cathy and Jack to impart the details, he had gleaned from the government office in Aberdeen.

"Cathy, you know how I said I was not keen on the long voyage I would have to go on to get to Savanta?"

"Yes, over two weeks you said." Replied Cathy.

"Well, you're not going to believe this but we're going to be flown out there."

The Spirit of St. Andrew

"Flown....my God. How come?"

"Thanks to Mr Hitler, that's how. He heard about all this 'cos he's friends with Phillipe Ramon in Beldovia. He's laying on planes, first, from Aberdeen to Frankfurt, then from there to the west tip of Africa, then on across the Atlantic to Beldovia, no more than two days......brilliant!" Exclaimed Davie.

"Jesus, that sounds great Davie but, I noticed you said we."

"That's right, both Tam and I are allowed one guest with us.... I've decided to take Helen with me, after all she's studying German Spanish and history at Aberdeen university, never know what she might learn on a trip like that."

"That all sounds grand Davie, and when does this all happen?" Asked Jack.

"This is the excitin' bit Jacky boy.....next Thursday!"

Looma woke at first light and stretched her body. As she did, she felt the baby move and gave a contented smile. she felt refreshed if not a little hungry. Being a woman of the forest, she looked around for food but saw nothing, it was then she decided to press on. Before she went, she stood on the large stone again and gazed down the river. To her utter shock away in the distance she was sure she could see what looked like four tribesmen on the move towards her. "Huaorani!" she said to herself, before taking off.

The Spirit of St. Andrew

She didn't think they had spotted her, but she wanted to keep as much distance between them and herself as possible. She was confident that they would stop pursuing her after today, the Huaorani did not like to get too far away from their turf and they would know that not much further upriver would be the Kayapo and the Yanomami, and though not afraid of them, they would know they were just four men, not enough to repulse an attack.

Several times along the way Looma stopped to look back and sure enough, the Huaorani were closing in. The day was getting on and Looma was starting to tire. A little further on and she suddenly became aware of the sound of rushing water up ahead, "the waterfall" she whispered to herself.

She remembered clearly on the way down that this was where she injured her ankle, and it was concerning her as to how she was going to transverse this obstacle. She knew she couldn't climb the side of the fall, and trying to travel around it would take her away from the river perhaps causing her to get lost just like the girl who ran off trying to get back to Maboosh of the Kayapo tribe.

She was starting to feel uneasily aware that the hunting pack was close behind and it was time to decide, climb the fall or go into the jungle.

It was then that she noticed that the water didn't fall straight down but poured out away from the rocks. There was a gap in behind the fall that she may get through and across to the other side where she wanted to be anyway.

The Spirit of St. Andrew

More to the point though, she could hide there until the Huaorani were away.

As she had hoped there was a ledge she could sidle along, although it was very narrow. Looma was very apprehensive about going under the fall until she looked back and saw the Huaorani within 100 yards of where she was. She didn't think they had seen her yet but before they did, she decided to go for it.

Under she went, the noise of the water blanked out any other sound from the rainforest and was quite intimidating. The ledge was no wider than her foot, in fact she could curl her toes around it and get more grip. As she edges slowly along, she suddenly became aware of four flickering shimmering shapes approaching the waterfall, it was the search party, and they were upon her.

Above the sound of the water rushing, she could make out that there were people talking loudly so they could hear each other above the sound of the fall. It soon became apparent to Looma that one of them was being sent along to where she was.

Looma, now around three quarters of the way across, realised she had reached a point where there was a gap in the rock, a small alcove, and she decided to hide there as the native was bound to see her as soon as he set off. She didn't know what she was hoping for, probably that the man making the crossing would perhaps slip and fall before he reached her or look and see nothing and just turn back.

The Spirit of St. Andrew

The Huaorani who was making his way along very gingerly was indeed the man Looma had been paired with, this probably the reason the other men sent him. He was very uncomfortable on his journey; his feet were bigger that Looma's and he wasn't getting the grip that she had.

Looma started to breath heavily as she became aware of the man's approach. Firstly, she saw his arm as he was almost upon her. Her eyes widened as he turned his head around the bend only for then to stare at each other wondering what to do next. Looma didn't hesitate, as soon as his shoulder was visible to her, she pushed him into the cascading water. He went over screaming like a child. Looma knew few, if any of the Huaorani could swim, and that she had more than likely sent him to his death.

She could see the shadowy figures of the rest of the search party looking to the waters to see if their accomplice was going to surface. She was also hoping they were assuming he had slipped and fallen to his death and that they would leave.

She waited quite a while, long enough to see the remaining three head back down river.

It was with a sigh of relief that she reached the other side of the fall. As she looked back sure enough the three Huaorani were well on their way back home. Suddenly she took another look down stream and was sure she could see the body of her late man lying motionless between two large stones. She then said words in Yanomami to the effect of, "good riddance".

Looma was aware of the time of year and what fruits were available within the rainforest. She didn't want to venture too far in, but it wasn't long before she happened on some berries and nuts and ate hungrily.

As she pressed on, she was now aware that she was inside Kayapo territory and had to be vigilant. Again, she had large stones to walk over as she kept on a pace. Light was starting to fade and once more she looked for a place to rest up for the night. Once again, a fallen tree seemed to be the best situation although it was hanging out over the river. She knew that if she went out on to the large bushy tree and settled in between a couple of its large branches she would be well hidden should an early morning hunting party happen by.

As she made her way along the trunk of the tree, she became aware of a squeaking noise up ahead. As she raised her head to look forward, she noticed a puma cub about four feet in front of her. She smiled at its cuteness. It didn't seem too keen on Looma though, as it hissed towards her.

The little cat then seemed to give out a calling sound which it seemed to aim at something behind her. Looma turned herself around slowly only to find herself staring into the yellow eyes of the biggest Puma she had ever seen, and it did not look at all happy.

The Spirit of St. Andrew

As quick as a flash, Looma stretched out her arms and grabbed the kitten, spun around and laid it in front of the mother cat. The big cat crouched down and hissed seemingly unsure of how to handle what just taken place. She knew she couldn't spring at Looma for fear of knocking her kitten into the river. Looma moved slowly up the tree away from the now reunited cats. She breathed the biggest sigh of relief as the mother picked up the kitten in her mouth and walk of back down from the tree.

When Looma awoke the next morning, she knew she was now within a day of reaching her own people and was excited at the prospect. She had only seconds before left the large tree when she became aware of voices and movement up ahead. "Kayapo", she said to herself. She looked around for somewhere to hide but could see no realistic cover. The voices and undergrowth rustling were closing in.

Before she knew it, she found herself going into the river. The flow was not too rapid as she decided to cling close to the side and hoped she would not be spotted as she crouched into the embankment. The voices of the hunting party were now right on top of her as she clung as closely as she could to the overhanging grass. One voice was familiar to Looma, it was Maboosh, the oversized leader of the Kayapo. He was as close to Looma now as she had ever been to him, in fact, glancing upwards, she could see Maboosh's toes, sticking out over the side of the river directly above her.

Looma thought for sure they would see her, but to her amazement and relief they soon moved away and disappeared into the undergrowth. She was also pleased to see that they had moved away in a direction opposite to the one she was heading in.

Later that day, to her utter delight, Looma saw some of her people working at the riverside and she rushed forward to fall into their embrace.

CHAPTER 25.
FLYING HIGH.

Because he had flown before, Davie was telling Helen about all the possible things that could happen, as their flight had them halfway across the North Sea on their way to Frankfurt in Germany.

"You know Helen, this Adolf Hitler guy seems like a nice bloke laying on these flights for us." Said Davie.

"Em Dad, you really do need to read a bit more. If you did, you would find out that this "nice bloke" you talk about, is a total dictator who rules with a fist of iron. The way he is treating the Jewish people in Germany is terrible, he closes all their business's removes them from their homes to God knows where......"

Davie cuts in, "Och! Helen, if you believe all you hear, you'll eat all you see. I think that's just stories from other countries to put people against him."

"You are unbelievable Dad, have you forgotten already what you saw in Beldovia and how they treated you.........Phillipe Ramon is just like Hitler Dad."

The Spirit of St. Andrew

Davie hesitated for a moment, "Anyway......" he went on, "........I'm only going for the money that bast......sorry, tyrant, owes me and Tam for what he put us through."

"Well said dad, and I'm only going to keep you company, brush up on my languages.......and see a bit of the world." said Helen, with a broad smile.

The Junker JU-52 plane Hitler had laid on soon landed in Frankfurt, firstly to refuel, and to allow passengers to stretch their legs.

While in the airport, some officials approached Davie and Helen to see that all was well with their flight. As they spoke a bustle arose at the other end of the terminal as people started to gather around what Davie thought was some dignitary or another entering the building.

To their amazement the female official who was with them went on to say that the Fuhrer Mr Hitler had been diverted to Frankfurt and wanted to meet the people who were off to Beldovia at his expense.

It was a little frightening for Davie and Helen as everyone Hitler passed on his way towards them raised their arms in salute to their master, none daring to turn away.

Davie and Helen felt a little intimidated as Adolf Hitler and his entourage closed in on them. The first thing that struck them both was just how small he was, Davie figured about 5'8".

The Spirit of St. Andrew

The female official, a tall, blonde, very attractive woman, introduced the couple to her Fuehrer who then spoke to her in German, which to Hitler's astonishment Helen answered in German.

Hitlers eyes widened, seemingly surprised by Helen's response.

Davie then tugged at Helens coat whispering "What did he say?"

"He wants to know if your flight is alright?"

"I told him yes.......and thank him very much." Said Helen to a somewhat shocked Davie.

Hitler nodded then spoke again.

"He wishes to know what you will spend all the money on?" Said Helen to her Dad.

Before Davie could speak, Helen cut in, "Well..." She said, in clear German ".... we plan to donate some of it to the new Jewish community which has sprung up in our city due to the amount of them arriving from Europe."

Everyone froze momentarily on hearing Helen's words.

Almost as soon as she had spoken Hitler's demeanour dropped as he glowered at Mary before gathering himself, nodded to the two of them then turned and left.

"What the hell did you say to him?" demanded Davie.

"Oh, I just told him we would help the Jewish community in Aberdeen with the money!"

"Helen! What the fuck made you say that.... I mean there is no Jewish community in Aberdeen for God's sake, at least not that I know of?" Demanded Davie.

"Sorry dad, just couldn't stop myself."

"Jesus......." Continued Davie, ".... I wouldn't be surprised if he's cancelled our bloody flight after that, and you do know as well that we have to come back this way."

"Don't be daft dad, the man knows that would only set him in a bad light if he did." Replied Helen confidently.

As it was their flight did leave and it was on to the tip of West Africa where once again the plane refuelled before setting of on the longest part of the flight across the Atlantic Ocean to Beldovia.

On arrival they were taken through the streets of Savanta to the presidential palace. On the way, Davie was fascinated by the numbers of common people who had taken to the streets in seeming protest. He remembered being told that Ramon had a vice-like grip on the people and any kind of protest was quickly quashed. This, it seemed was bigger than anything of the past and their car was having a bit of trouble making its way through with some people banging on the roof of the car.

When they arrived at the palace there were quite a few press photographers snapping away, Phillipe Ramon wanted the world to see what a merciful and generous leader he was.

Suddenly, a very familiar face caught Davies eye, it was Tam, and he rushed over and embraced his great friend. Not just Tam, but there was his brother Wull, there as Tam's guest.

Once they had all greeted each other they were quickly escorted further into the palace where none other than President Ramon was stood waiting with his wife and other dignitaries to greet them. On their approach Davie was surprised that Ramon was even smaller that Adolf Hitler and could only be about 5'6" tall. Davie wasn't surprised when Tam leaned over to him and said, "What a fuckin' wee midget!"

After the introductions Phillipe Ramon ranted on in Spanish, which Helen was trying her hardest to translate to her Dad. As camera flashes popped, he was telling the world what a wonderful person he was, causing Davie and Tam grimace at the thought

He then approached the lads and handed them what seemed to be a couple of cheques. They were then informed by the translator that it was a token gesture and that the money had already been forwarded to their bank accounts back home while they were in transit.

Like Hitler before him, he then asked what they would do with such a large sum of money. When the translator finished Davie immediately swung round to Helen and stared hard at her as if to say, "don't you dare!"

After basically saying they would invest it in their future, the president then asked what they would like to do or see, while they were here.

Once this was translated Helen, as quick as a flash said, "The "Hellhole"! Which caused a ripple of laughter.

"Helen, don't be daft, surely you'd rather see the Aztec ruins and temples?" Said her father with a forced smile.

"No... not really.......?" Quizzed Helen, "......after all the "hellhole" is where they almost killed you......I want to see this place."

It was then that Wull butted in, "Actually, I wouldn't mind seeing it myself."

"Jesus......" Said Tam, ".......are you two a couple of morbid bastards or what!"

Davie could see that the president was being told what they had requested, and a smile formed across his face. Then his translator spoke.

"President Ramon sees no reason why you should not see where your father was incarcerated and will arrange for a flight out this afternoon before your return home tomorrow."

After another crowd infested ride through the city, they were soon on their way on the plane that had taken Tam and Davie to the "hellhole" just under one year before only this time it was just the four of them, the pilot and a prison guard. The difference with this journey to the airfield and the one before, is that the lads were sure that they had heard gunfire in the distance and wondered just what the hell was going on in Savanta.

Helen was as fascinated by the extent of the rainforest as her father had been when he first set eyes on it.

"My God dad, just look at the size of this place......how in hell did you and Tam make your way out of such a vastness?"

"Well Helen, do you see that river winding its way southeast......" Said Davie pointing out of the window, "........that was our passage to freedom."

"Wow!" Exclaimed a very impressed young lady.

Helen then spoke quietly to her dad, "Listen Dad, I want to thank you for taking me on this......well.......adventure, and I'm so glad I chose the "hellhole" to visit rather than some ancient ruin."

"I'm glad you're enjoying this, but I can assure you I'll be happy when we are away to hell out o' this place."

Helen just grinned before slumping back in her seat and enjoying the flight.

Looma had been back with her people only two weeks when she gave birth to a little boy. Although a little early, the baby was fine and Looma had named him Tam, after his father.

The condition of the Yanomami within the shabono was a little apprehensive as word was being spread by passing natives that Maboosh of the Kayapo tribe was raiding other encampments of the rainforest and the Yanomami may be next. He was obviously "power hungry" and acting out of character for a leader of a native rainforest people. The Yanomami knew that the number of men he now had following him made him far too powerful to be repelled by them.

Sure enough, one morning they all arose to find themselves encircled by the Kayapo and being ordered to surrender or die!

As the plane circled to land, they all noticed that the prisoners were nowhere to be seen and must therefore be shut in their huts. As the plane taxied to the gate Captain Sanchez seemed to have formed a guard of honour for his guests, this probably being the reason the prisoners were all locked up.

Tam and Davie noticed that three new huts had been erected just outside the perimeter of the camp and some people were milling around outside, including to their surprise, three children who looked no older than 12 years. It would seem Captain Sanchez didn't consider them of any danger to his new guests.

The Spirit of St. Andrew

They walked together to the gate where Sanchez was waiting with an outstretched hand toward Davie and Tam. Davie shook him hand but a reluctant Tam hesitated for a second before responding.

Tam leaned towards Davie and whispered, "I really wanted to smack him right in the puss."

As Captain Sanchez was about to greet Helen and Wull, everyone was taken by surprise when the guard who had flown with them, suddenly removed his pistol from his side, grabbed the pilot around the neck from behind and pointed the gun to his temple.

All the other guards as well as Sanchez made for their guns as everyone took a step back and gazed in amazement.

The man shouted out in Spanish along the lines of "leave your guns alone or I shoot this man."

Sanchez signalled for the guards to step back before he asked the man what he wanted.

Continuing in Spanish he made his statement, he said, "the revolution had begun in Savanta and he wanted the immediate release of Carlos Vegas their leader".

Davie was holding a now trembling Helen close to him as all this was transpiring, as he did the noise of unhappy men banging on the walls of their huts became apparent. Something was going to give!

The Spirit of St. Andrew

To everyone's amazement the pilot them grabbed the guard's arm which held the pistol and started to wrestle with him. To everyone's horror the gun went off and the pilot lay motionless to the ground, blood spurting from his neck.

In an instant the other guards were all over the assailant, forcing him to the ground before cuffing him. The camp medical team were soon on the scene, but it was too late for the pilot who lay dead on the ground.

"Jesus......" Said Wull, "…. what the hell just happened?"

"Please......" Demanded Sanchez, "……...everyone keep calm we now have this situation under control." He then indicated to his guards to go and calm the prisoners down.

"Captain, I'm not so sure everything is under control. We have seen a lot of people on the streets of Savanta before we came here, something was happening…….and now this!" Said Davie.

"Please...." Said captain Sanchez, "…….we must remain calm, I will telegraph Savanta to see what is happening…….wait here everyone."

It was then that Tam piped up, "You might want to ask about a new pilot being flown out as well?"

"Si...si.." He said, as he walked off.

Davies party all went and sat in the canteen area just as it started to pour down with rain. There they would wait for Sanchez to return. He was away about half an hour and, when he arrived, he sat down ashen faced, before speaking.

"It seems that Savanta is under siege by a band of revolutionaries. They have taken over the airport and are not allowing any flights out or into the capitol. The only flight they allowed out was your German Junker 52, with a message to Hitler to leave Beldovia alone from now on."

"That's all very well captain but how in the name of fuck do we get out of here?........." Was Tam's terse request, "......I mean are there any other pilots inside this place?"

"Drug dealers, vagabonds, thieves, murderers aplenty, but I'm afraid no pilots, signor."

Davie then piped up with a surprise comment, "I know where there's a pilot!"

"What?" Said a rather amazed looking Helen.

"Jesus......of course." Replied Tam.

"What the hell are you two talking about?" Demanded Wull.

"Charles Porteous is holed up with the Yanomami not that very far from here, the man's a pilot." Said Davie.

"Just what are you suggesting Dad?" Demanded Helen, a troubled look on her face.

"I'm not suggestin' anything, just stating a fact." Replied Davie.

"But how do you know he's still there, I mean he could have died, or taken off, or been taken by that other tribe you spoke about...." Said Helen.

"Well..." Said Tam, "......it seems to me that the only way we are going to get to hell out of here is to get someone to fly us out in that aeroplane, and the only pilot in the vicinity is good old Charie and I for one am off to fetch him."

"Count me in as well Tam." Said Davie, who then turned to Helen and Wull.

"We've got to try this, or we could be here for God knows how long and we don't know what kind of a state those prisoners are going to get in once they find out all what's happening in Savanta. Wull, I know you'd come in a second, but I need you to look after Mary for me...can you do that?"

"Of course." Replied Wull.

Davie and Tam were soon readying themselves, as they did captain Sanchez approached Davie and Tam and gave them a waterproof poncho each which they slipped over their shoulders. He then handed Davie a revolver in a holster which he fixed around his waist.

"Good God...." He said, "......I feel like that cowboy actor John Wayne."

Davie and Tam looked at each other in a way that said, ready?

Helen gave her dad a hug, "You be bloody careful Davie Harley."

Captain Sanchez then took them aside, "You will have to go upstream a bit where the water is shallower, and you can cross......"

"Aye...." Said Tam, "......well, we weren't plannin' on makin' the jump we made the last time we departed your company captain."

The captain ignored Tam, "I don't think you gentlemen have thought this right through, alright, you can maybe get a pilot, but where on earth are you going to fly to, Savanta is closed, they'll have barricades up?"

"Mr Sanchez we will cross that bridge once we get our pilot, I'm sure he'll have ideas on where to go. In the meantime I'd be grateful if you were to fuel up the plane for a long journey." Said Davie as he started off, to which Sanchez nodded.

They told them all that they would hope to be back within 24 to 36 hours. One of the guards handed them a canteen of water and a small parcel of food which they tucked into the bag that Sanches had given them, and they were off.

Wading across the river was a new one for the lads. The water was up to their waist and was flowing at a moderate pace. It was around 60ft across where they were, and they were having to watch their footing as there were stones and gravel underfoot, furthermore the heavy falling rain seemed even this early, to be upping the flow of the water.

The Spirit of St. Andrew

Davie was leading and was about ten feet from the other side when Tam gave out a roar as his feet went from under him. Davie wasn't near enough to grab Tam as he slowly started to move downstream. Davie was quickly out of the water and was shouting to Tam to try and get on to his feet again, but Davie could see the current was too strong to let him do this, Tam was heading for the waterfall.

Davie then went into a run as he realised, he had to get ahead of his friend before he went over. Now, Davie knew Tam could probably survive going over the fall if there were no jagged rocks at the bottom, or that he didn't get caught up in a vortex under the force of the water and drown.

Looking ahead he could see that there was a large, rounded rock at the edge of the start of the fall and he had to get there before Tam went over. He could see he was now ahead of his friend and started to unbuckle the gun holster the captain gave him to use as something for Tam to grab hold of and be pulled into the side.

Davie laid the revolver on a rock behind the one he was going to go on to. He then threw himself flat on the rock and slung the holster out towards Tam just as he came towards him.

"Gotcha!" Exclaimed Davie as Tam grabbed the holster buckle. Davie pulled with all his might to get Tam ashore before he went over. Davie knew he would have to let Tam go if he did go over the fall because he would never hold his weight with the force of the waterfall on him as well.

As it was Tam scrambled on to the large rock, then lay on his back to gather himself.

"Way hay! We did it!" Shouted Davie as he embraced Tam when he stood up. As they did so Tam staggered about trying to be as happy as Davie was. As they embraced and danced around Davie without thinking kicked the pistol over the edge of the fall. Tam watched with disbelief as the gun landed in a large pool at the side of the fall.

"Fuck!" Shouted Davie, before gathering himself. "Och, who needs a gun anyway we're just goin' tae get Charlie boy and get out of there."

The lads were making good time as they pressed on. They remembered when they first made the journey that eventually led to the Yanomami Shabono and had covered the ground many times while out hunting with Laurel and Hardy. Now of course they knew the direct route and felt confident of being there in two to three hours.

"By God Davie, I never had us down for being back in this God forsaken place." Said Tam as he ploughed on behind his friend.

"Nor me Tam, nor me."

As they eventually approached the encampment that was the Yanomami Shabono, the lads were surprised that there were no children or outside activities going on.

The Spirit of St. Andrew

Normally at this time of day all sorts of work would be being undertaken.

"Hold on Tam....something's no right here." Said Davie, as he held out a stopping hand to his friend.

"Far to bloody quite for my liking Davie." Replied Tam.

As they crouched down behind a large shrub, they were suddenly aware of someone behind them. Sure enough, as they turned, they were confronted by four spear bearing Kayapo Indians who were gesturing for them to move forward into the Shabono.

As they entered the compound, they were greeted by cheering Kayapo natives who were watching over the Yanomami people entrapped within the Shabono shelter.

Suddenly one of the native girls broke ranks and rushed forward towards the two lads, it was Looma, shouting "Tam....Tam!" as she threw her arms around him before the Kayapo could stop her.

"Looma!" Exclaimed Tam, utter shock in his voice, "What the fuck are you going here......how did you get here?"

It was then that a familiar voice spoke up from behind, "More to the point gentlemen, what the fuck are you doing here?" Asked Charles Porteous as a couple of Kayapo braves tried to push him back.

The Spirit of St. Andrew

"Long story……." Said Davie, about to explain when a tall figure approached from the back and stopped him, it was Maboosh.

He immediately started rambling on in Kayapo speak, as natives started rushing about to his commands, the first of these being to tie up Davie and Tam. Although he seemed to be circling in on Tam in particular.

Davie leaned into Charles, "Any idea what he's saying Charlie?"

"There is some similarities in the language but I'm not too sure. It seems he remembers Tam as the man with the gun who shot one of his men in the thigh." Said Charles.

"What's he likely to do?" Continued Davie.

"Davie I'm afraid that Maboosh had this crazy form of execution which he demonstrated yesterday on one of his men who tried to betray him and he's inferring using it on Tam."

"What....the murderin' bastard!" Exclaimed a rather irate Davie.

"Please, my friend……" Said Charles holding Davie back, "……he will only turn on you next."

"So, what's this form of execution then?"

"It's death by poison dart.... watch!" Said Charles.

Tam was struggling with the three men that were detaining him, one on each of his arms, and one behind with an arm around Tam's throat. Also being physically restrained was Looma who was screaming and shout for Tam's release.

It soon became obvious to Davie what was happening, a form of medieval firing squad with poison darts. Two of Mabosh's men stood about five yards back from Tam and aimed blow pipes in his direction as he was held by the three men. Maboosh raised his arm then lowered it quickly as if a signal to fire. Within a second two darts were lodged in Tam's chest as he slumped down on to his knees. A silence fell over the place as Maboosh gave a signal for Tam to be dragged away and dumped into the rainforest, there to the mercy of the wildlife.

Davies blood was now boiling as he too had to be restrained. All the Yanomami as well as Charles and Davie were ushered into the enclosed area of the Shabono held in by an encirclement of Kayapo natives. Looma was inconsolable as she was held by her mother.

Soon darkness fell, the Kayapo feasted at the fire usually prepared by the Yanomami. Davie and Charles sat together trying to figure out ways to get rid of Maboosh and his men. It was while they sat that Looma approached, babe in arms and held the small boy out to Davie.

"What's this?" Asked a surprised Davie.

"This Davie, is Tam's son, young Tam......" Said Charles, "......this amazing young woman escaped the clutches of the Huaorani and made her way all the way back up the river to here, where she gave birth to this little fellow."

As Davie held the small bundle, he felt himself having to fight back a tear as he thought of the fate of his friend and the fact that he hadn't seen his little son.

That night Davie proceeded to fill Charles in on all that had happened, right up to the killing of the pilot.

"Sure Davie, I could fly the plane but with Savana a no-go, there is only one place I can think of within distance of the "hellhole" ...." Said Charles.

"And where is that?" Asked an attentative Davie.

"Belem of Para on the mouth of the Amazon in Brazil, Rio is way too far my friend. On the plus side, Belem is a large city with a good-sized harbour for shipping. Many boats come and go." Said Charles.

"Aye..." Said Davie, ".... come and go to Britian ah hope."

"On the plus side as well my friend, there is no one after Charles Porteous in Belem." Said Charles with a smile.

"All this is fine Charles and sounds like a good plan but first, we have to get to hell away from these damned Kayapo and Maboosh!"

The rain soon stopped as both Yanomami and Kayapo sheltered within the Shabono. Davie felt disgust and anger towards Maboosh and his followers and was determined to try and find a way to get at them if he could and gain revenge for his friend.

It was very early morning, barely light, when Davie and the others were awakened by Kayapo braves remonstrating towards Maboosh who rose to see what the fuss was about. Most of the Kayapo had gathered in a group where some were pointing towards the undergrowth. Now even Davie and the other were curious and went forward to see for themselves.

There for all to see on the edge of the rainforest was a large dark, almost completely black figure of perhaps a man or maybe some other kind of creature. It was stood still with two whites of eyes staring towards the Shabono. The eyes looked eerie against the black face as they seemed to home in on Maboosh. Suddenly the creature raised its arms above its head, leaned back and gave of the almightiest roar it could muster. Almost everyone took a step back when this happened. It then lowered its arms and pointed towards the Shabono and shout from the top of its voice, "MABOOOOOSH".

"What the fuck is that?" Demanded Charles, as he turned to Davie, where another surprise awaited him, for Davie Harley was smiling.

"Just look at the frame......who else has a frame that size Charlie?"

"No....it can't be!" Said a somewhat bewildered Charles.

Maboosh's men were apprehensive towards whatever it was, even when Maboosh ordered two of them to attack the creature.

Maboosh was now raging at his men for their reluctance to attack and started to threaten them.

Suddenly two of them attacked, rushing at the large black form which stood and waited. Waited for just the right time to raise an arm and point it towards the onrushing natives.

BANG! BANG! Two frighteningly loud shots wrang out from the dark figure and the two natives fell to the ground and never moved.

Maboosh was franticly trying to get other men to attack but they were all cowering away and falling back. He then grabbed one of his men and forced him to join Maboosh in an attack, as the creature slowly started to approach them.

With spears raised Maboosh and the other native attacked only to be met with the same outcome.

BANG! BANG! Once more two shots wrang out, and once more two Kayapo fell to the ground and never moved. This time, one of them was Maboosh!

On seeing their great leader fall dead nearby them, the rest of the Kayapo made a dash for the undergrowth towards their own village. At almost the same time the Yanomami men, led by Lor and Hor, went after the Kayapo natives, throwing spears and firing arrows after them.

The tall figure then drew his hands across his face to wipe away the mud which covered it, and, just as Davie had thought the face of Tomas Goodison appeared to everyone.

Looma was the first to dash forward and embrace Tam who hugged her in return, covering her with mud at the same time.

"What in the name of fuck just happened Tam?" Demanded Davie, who went on, "I mean we all thought the darts had killed you.......and the gun? Where the hell did you get the gun?"

"Davie, you forget, I survived being poisoned by a dart before, must have given me some kind of an immunity to it. So, I played dead, oh, I felt a bit dizzy and week, but I soon realised I was ok."

"But the gun?" Quizzed Charles.

"While I was figuring out what to do, I remembered the gun going over the fall and I saw where it landed. I headed back through the night and dived in for the gun. As I came up the embankment, I found myself covered in this black sticky mud stuff. The rain had made it worse from the time we went up the embankment Davie. I knew it made me look a bit fearsome if you like. Just as I thought the rain would wash it off it faired up. I thought

The Spirit of St. Andrew

about washing it off then again, I thought, this could scare the bejesus out o' these bastards.......what do you think?"

"No just the Kayapo, ye scared the bejesus oot o' us as well." Joked Davie.

CHAPTER 26.
A FLIGHT TO FREEDOM.

Everyone back at the penitentiary were surprise to see a young woman carrying a baby when Davie and Tam returned along with Charles Porteous.

Helen was particularly taken by the little infant and congratulated Tam on his parenthood. Tam explained that he had lost Looma before trying to get out of this country and failed. He was not about to do the same again and she was coming with them. The two were aware as well that a fair skinned child would always be slightly vilified within the rainforest communities and the baby would be best off with Looma and Tam in a new life. For his part Tam was determined to get back to the states where a dark-skinned child and mother are not quite such a standout.

Captain Sanchez informed the lads that the situation in Savanta had escalated while they were away, and a state of near civil war was ensuing. He told them that there was a lot of unrest within the penitentiary as prisoners were becoming very restless as news started to filter through to them about the ongoing situation.

"I suggest you gentlemen get away from here as quickly as you can......" Said Sanchez, "......I have seen to it that the plane is fully fuelled up and ready to go."

All seven of them were soon in the air and heading for Belem of Para in Brazil. On arrival they were treated well by the Brazilian authorities and were soon into a taxi and heading for the centre of the city.

Everyone received quite a shock as they drove along by the harbour and Davie shouted for the car to stop.

"Do you see that Tam?" Asked Davie.

"What......a load o' ships!"

"Aye and look at the one in the middle in front o' us." Demanded Davie.

"Jesus......" Said Tam, ".......The "Santa Margaretta", would you believe it. I wonder if good old Captain Brown is still in command?"

"I think we need to find out and see where he's headin' off to." said Davie.

As fate would have it the Saint Margaret was heading for the west coast of Africa before going on to Portugal. Davie soon contacted Captain Brown and once more agreed to work his and Helen's passage to Portugal where they would be able to contact the British embassy and obtain transport back to Aberdeen.

As for Tam, Looma, wee Tam and Wull, it turned out that Wull had contacts who were able to arrange a flight back to the United States.

Charles Porteous, no one knew just what became of him! Perhaps he made his way back to the Yanomami. Perhaps he got back into aviation. Perhaps!

Phillipe Raman was overthrown, and a democratic government took over.

Through the money they received, Davie was able to invest in the farm and went into partnership with Cathy and Jack. Tam also invested in Wulls tobacco company and went on to have two more children with looma who took to a western lifestyle like a duck to water.

The only downside to all of this was the real threat of war with Adolf Hitler starting to invade neighbouring countries in Europe.

On the farm, Davie had students from Aberdeen helping with the harvest some of whom were from Holland and were concerned about the welfare of their families, problem being that they were Jewish.

To be continued...

ABOUT THE AUTHOR

B

I was born not far from Aberdeen in a town called Banchory in 1948. My family moved south to the Dundee area where I received a basic primary and secondary school education which I left aged 15 with a secondary education certificate passing in 5 subjects.

Being one of five children I had to go out to work as soon as I left school to help put food on the table.

At the age of 23 I married the love of my life Helen, together we had three wonderful children (1girl 2 boys) who have between them supplied us with 4 wonderful grandchildren.

In my younger days my sole love (other than my wife and family) was playing football (soccer) where I played to a fairly high standard reaching junior level (one below senior level in Scotland) at my height.

I did not start to write until my family were all up and partnered off (around 55 years old). My inspiration came from stories my parents and grandparents related to me. My grandfather fought in the first world war and was the basis for my hero in "The Spirit Of St Andrew". My other grandfather worked a farm outside Banchory and was quite a character. As well as fathering his three children to his wife he had also fathered several other children outside of wedlock.

My mother Mary Donald was my early inspiration to write. As well as writing herself she was always at me to write down the stories we shared with each other.

I have in my time completed three fictional books, one four-part sitcom (Peggy's Place) a three-part children's story (Libby and the amazing garden shed) and have written many poems. At present I am collecting material for the follow on to "The Spirit of SBt Andrew).